The Butler's Son

by

Geoff Hill

THUNDERCHILD PUBLISHING
Huntsville, Alabama

This is a work of fiction. All of the characters, organizations, and events portrayed in this novel are either products of the author's imagination or are used fictitiously.

The Butler's Son

Edited by Dan Thompson

ISBN-13: 978-1537673608
ISBN-10: 1537673602

Published by Thunderchild Publishing.
Find us at http://www.ourworlds.net/thunderchild/

Table of Contents

Chapter One

July, 1914. Termon estate, County Tyrone

Max Edwards was eighteen when he saw the woman he loved, and the man he wanted to kill.

He was walking along the path down to the lake with Fido when he rounded the ancient oak and came face to face with Major Martin, the owner of Termon.

"Back from Japan, sir?" said Max.

"Evidently," said the Major, taking the cigar from his mouth. "Worst year of my life, although it had its…rewards." He looked at the woman beside him.

"Kumiko, this is young Max, the butler's son. Max, this is Kumiko, my wife."

She was tiny, and slender as a reed, with a face like a slightly amused elf, but the most remarkable thing about her was the colour of her eyes: a flickering, iridescent green the colour of rainwashed meadows in spring.

"Good evening, Max," she bowed.

Max bowed back.

"Konbanwa, Kumiko-san," he said.

Her eyes widened, then smiled.

"Don't be surprised," said the Major. "He's read every book in the library."

They walked on, and Max watched them go; the Major in his uniform and Sam Browne belt, bearing his moustache before him and trailing an air of cigar smoke and superiority behind.

And Kumiko, seeming to float beside him in a lilac kimono with a burnt orange sash.

"Gosh, Fido," said Max.

"Arf," said Fido, who as a collie always had to have the last word.

Max watched them disappear out of sight along the woodland walk to the back of the big house, then looked back at the lake, with its ragged island and the setting sun beyond.

Then he walked past the sawmill and the hay barn, emerged opposite the door to the walled garden, and turned left past the outhouses, through the archway into the big yard.

Through another archway, he turned left again, opened the door and climbed the stone steps to the rooms above the coach house where he lived with his parents.

In the living room, he found his mother stirring a pot of Irish stew on the range, and hugged her, drinking in her smell of warm hay and salad cream.

"Hello, son. Cup of tea? Your father should be home soon after he's finished serving dinner," she said, wiping her hands on her apron and rescuing a stray strand of hair which had fallen over her forehead.

Max sat down to read a two day-old *Belfast Telegraph*, which made its way from the big house via Mrs Rapier the cook to his father and hence to him, and had just got to the sports pages when he heard the scullery door slamming, and looked out of the tall sash window to see the familiar sight of his father striding across the yard whistling, a copy of not only the previous day's *Telegraph*, but the weekly *Tyrone Constitution* tucked under the arm of his black three-piece suit.

"That stew smells good, Maria. As always," said Robert, kissing her on the cheek then loosening his tie and settling into the armchair with the *Con*.

"I met the young Madam by the lake with the Major earlier, father," said Max.

"Yes, she's very striking, isn't she? Quite a lovely person. It seems she was his interpreter when he was in Japan. An orphan, by all accounts," said his father.

"She must be only twenty. Far too young to be married," said his mother.

"Ha! You're one to talk," smiled his father.

"She is a poppet, though. Her hair's like blackberries at midnight," said Maria.

"What a lovely expression, Maria," said Robert. "You should have been a poet."

"Too busy making stew, sadly," said Maria.

"Shall we continue the game after dinner, father?" said Max.

"Why not? Where were we?"

"You were just about to lose your queen, in which case there would be little point in continuing."

"Very funny. I remember the days when I used to beat you."

The next morning, Max went for a long walk down the Glen with Fido, then back past the Druid's Stone, a strange triangular construction of giant slabs of granite, and found Mrs Rapier in the kitchen bending over a steaming pot of tomato and basil soup.

"Max, you wouldn't be a dear and get me a bag of flour from McGarrity's?" she said.

"Of course, Cook," said Max, lifting the lid on another pot and finding her famous Oxford marmalade bubbling away.

"Want to try these and tell me what you think?" said Cook.

"Love to," said Max, getting two spoons from the cutlery drawer.

"Soup's yum, and marmalade's double yum," he said after.

"Spot on," said Cook.

Max washed and dried the spoons, then crossed the small yard, collected his knapsack from his bedroom, and went to get his bicycle from the room beside the stables in the big yard.

"You going up to Carrickmore, Max?" said Willie Magee the farrier. "Any chance of a bag of hoof nails from Rafferty's?"

"And a gross of six-inches?" said Alan Kilpatrick the carpenter from the top of a ladder where he was fixing a joist.

"Flipping heck. I'll be charging my usual delivery fee, of course," said Max.

"Naturally. Bugger all from me, and bugger all squared from Alan," said Willy Magee.

Max laughed, then cycled out of the big yard and took the back lane, past the door into the walled garden in which Willy Magee the gardener and young Willy Magee the gardener's son had been busy for days picking gooseberries, strawberries and raspberries.

He leaned the bicycle against the wall and found them in the hothouse, drinking tea. The air was rich and dank with the smell of growth.

"Going up to Carrickmore, Max?" said young Willy.

"Aye. Need anything?"

"Don't think so. Dad?"

"Don't think so," said his father.

"Glad to hear it. I don't think my knapsack could have taken much more."

"Want some gooseberries for Seamus McGarrity?"

"Aye, can do."

Young Willy got up, wrapped a handful in a muslin bag, and handed them over.

Max cycled on, past the back gate lodge then onto the main road past his old one-room primary school and up the curving hill into Carrickmore.

Rather than get the flour at McGarrity's then have to cycle up the hill to Rafferty's with it, he went to Rafferty's first, opening the door and stepping into the cavernous gloom which seemed to stretch back for ever, with shelves crammed with hardware on the right, everything from hams to bicycles hanging from the roof, and on the left a polished wooden counter behind which were stacked clothes, shoes and boots, all of it lit by skylights from which four columns of dusty light shafted down.

"Ah, young Master Edwards," said Pat Rafferty, emerging from a door behind the counter. "What'll it be?"

"A gross of six-inch nails and a bag of hoofs, please, Mr Rafferty," said Max. "On the Termon account."

At McGarrity's, the bell above the door tinged, and Seamus emerged from the back as Max stepped past the bags of spuds and turnips on the stone floor.

"Bag of flour for Cook, please, Mr McGarrity," said Max. "On account."

"Grand job," said Seamus, and measured the flour out from a hessian sack behind the counter, then looked back at the rows of glass sweetie jars behind him. "Like a handful of clove rock?"

"I'll take some brandy balls for father, thank you very much," said Max. "Oh, and here's some gooseberries from young Willy Magee. You'd be a fool to refuse them."

Seamus laughed.

"Yes, very funny. Too clever for my own good, you are."

Just for variety, Max cycled home by the front lane, past the gate lodge and the Water Meadow.

In the Devil's Wood, so called because it was supposed to be haunted, the wind whispered in the trees and the rooks cawed, as they always did. It was the sound of Termon.

Passing the Devil's Wood was all right in the day, but there were times when Max found himself cycling or walking just that little bit faster past it at night, then laughing at his foolishness.

As he cycled through the archway into the big yard, John Jameson the blacksmith was ringing the bell above the coach house for the workers to come in from the fields for their midday meal, and after Max had delivered his messages, he walked back out to where they were washing their faces and hands in the stream they called the Runner, or using the drop toilet in a little outhouse built over it downstream.

In the long stone room by the archway into the big yard, John's wife Margaret had already lit the open fireplace and swung a large black pot filled with potatoes over it.

The men sat themselves on wooden benches down each side of the room, and Margaret ladled the spuds onto used copies of the *Con* and the *Telegraph* on the floor in front of them, to be eaten in their hands, with salt and butter.

The pot was replaced by a kettle just as black and the tea was made. They lit their pipes, took a mug of sweet and milky tea, threw the leavings into the remains of the fire and returned to the fields.

Max watched them go, then went home to find his mother making vegetable soup.

"That smells delicious, mother. Would you like some meat to go with it?" said Max.

"That would be lovely, son. Will it be fresh?"

He laughed, and picked up his father's .22 rifle from where it leaned against the china cupboard.

"It'll still be twitching. Rabbit or pigeon?"

The next morning, he brought his mother in a cup of tea at half past six to find her still in bed, which wasn't like her.

"Are you all right, mother?"

"I'll be up in a minute, dear, but I seem to have come down with a bit of flu. Cold and shivery and aching all over."

"Do you want me to light the fires in the big house, Maria?" said Robert. "I can get up now and do it before I serve breakfast."

"I'll do it, father. You stay in bed and keep mother warm," said Max.

"Bless you, son," said his mother.

"Thank you, Max," said his father.

Max walked down the stone steps, then across the small yard and into the scullery and pantry, then through the kitchen and up seven stone steps into the dining room, which was dominated by a large William IV table, with a sideboard along one wall for serving dishes.

The fireplace was at the far end, flanked by two bell cords to summon the servants, and with a slightly gloomy portrait of the Rev Charles Cobbe Beresford, who had built Termon as his rectory in 1815 before it was bought by the Martins after the disestablishment of the Irish Church.

"Cheer up, chum. It may never happen," said Max, setting to work with paper and kindling.

Around him, the great house was still, and the only sound was the fizz and crack as the damp logs caught.

When it was blazing, he went through to the drawing room, with its hand-painted floral wallpaper which by all accounts had been there since the house was built.

Along one wall was a row of glass and mahogany cabinets, various sofas and armchairs were dotted around the room and beside the French windows looking out at the great oak tree in the middle of the lawn sat a Steinway & Sons grand piano, although Max could never remember hearing it played.

Above it was a painting of the Major's mother, a society beauty from Totnes who had died hours after giving birth to her only son.

He left the fire crackling nicely, then walked down the hall past the gun rack with its row of rifles, shotguns and ancient blunderbusses, then a collection of African spears and clubs which Major Martin's father had brought back from the Boer War not long before he too died, of malaria contracted in Komatipoort.

Next on the right was the library, Max's favourite room in the house, with a round table in the centre, comfortable club armchairs on either side of the fireplace and a little ante-room off it which was the Major's office. He lit the fire, then stood and looked at the books lining every wall.

"All life is here," he said, then went to one shelf, pulled out the Major's copy of A Japanese-English Reader, and memorised a few more phrases, as he did every morning.

"Anata wa watashitoisshoni ocha o toru nodeshou ka?" he said, several times over.

"Thank heavens it's atonal. Mandarin would be a bit of a pickle," he said, then put it back and picked out a copy of the poems of John Donne.

He was reading The Good-Morrow when a sound from upstairs indicated that the house was stirring.

He closed the book, put it back, and returned the way he had come.

* * *

A week later, he was forking manure into the rose beds with young Willy Magee the gardener's son on a scorching afternoon when he suddenly straightened.

"Is that the piano in the drawing room?" he said.

Willy stood, stretched his back and cocked an ear.

"Aye, it is. Dad said the Major's mother used to play it, but it hasn't been touched since."

Max stuck his fork in the manure pile and walked to the open French windows, listened for a few moments, then bent his head to look in.

Kumiko was sitting at the piano wearing an indigo kimono with a primrose yellow sash, and she stopped playing and looked up.

"Oh. Sorry, madam. I do apologise," said Max, suddenly aware that he was wearing an ancient pair of twill trousers and a frayed shirt with the sleeves rolled up.

"That is all right, Max. Were you enjoying it?" she said with a ghost of a smile.

"It was … enchanting. It's just that there is never music in the house. What was it?"

"Grieg," said Kumiko, and went back to playing.

Max stood there listening, then sighed, bowed his head and walked slowly back to forking manure.

Chapter Two

July 31, 1914

The annual Termon fete was in full swing, with a marquee set up on the edge of the lawn.

On one side, Max's father, out of his black suit for once and with his sleeves rolled up, was dispensing beer, home-made lemonade and ginger beer.

On the other, Cook was in her element behind a long table covered in white linen, on which a vast array of plates were piled high with cold roast beef, cold boiled beef, ribs of lamb, shoulders of lamb, roast fowls, roast ducks, a ham, a tongue, veal and ham pies, pigeon pies, Scotch eggs, boned and sliced chickens and capons, English cheeses, butter wrapped in lettuce leaves to keep it sweet and cool, fruit cake, Violet's fudge and strawberries and cream for afters, if anyone had any room left after that.

As always, Archie Close, the local eccentric from Drum Manor near Cookstown, where he lived in a state of chaos, had arrived in a jaunting car in full Highland dress and proceeded to march around the lawn playing his bagpipes until John Jameson had picked him up and carried him off, still playing, to laughter and applause.

"Not much point being on the other team than John, is there?" said young Willy Magee afterwards as they looked at the giant figure of Jameson wrap the rope around his waist as the tug of war anchor.

"Not really," said Max, and so it proved.

"Oh well," said Willy. "At least I won the cricket ball throwing contest."

"And the Major didn't take the broken greenhouse pane out of your pay," said Max, as John's son Adam came up.

"Willy, Dad says time for another Punch and Judy show," he said. "And bags I be Punch this time."

At the end of each table, a simple, beautiful flower display by Kumiko stood in a vase, and after the Punch and Judy, she gave a puppet show to the children of the estate.

It told the story of Kichiza, a page boy, and his sweetheart Oshichi, whose love finally overcomes their parents' attempts to marry them off to someone else.

The children sat around her, enthralled, and they were not alone, until Max's father called for him to bring out some more ginger beer.

He took one last look, then walked to the house.

That evening, the major and minor gentry of Tyrone toiled up the front and back lanes, most in jaunting cars or in a pair of charabancs the Major had organised in Omagh, although Briggs the solicitor made great play of arriving in a new Model T Ford. Then almost tripped and went head over heels getting out of it.

Violet tittered, and earned a rare stern look from Max's father, now back in his usual three-piece black suit.

The furniture in the drawing room had been pushed back against the walls, and as the string quartet played Mozart and the great and the good waltzed behind him, Max stood in front of the French windows and looked out at the children of the estate draped over the great oak in the middle of the lawn like ragged baubles, looking in at a world which was forever denied to them.

Standing between both worlds and uncertain which one he belonged in, he waved, and they all waved back, then laughed as little Annie Jameson, John and Margaret's daughter, waved so hard that she fell from the bottom branch.

She jumped up, none the worse for wear, and gave him her best smile.

"Heavens, quite the guest list for dinner tonight," said Max's father the following morning, looking at the sheet of paper in his hand. "Churchill, First Lord of the Admiralty, no less, our friends Carson and Craig fresh from saving us all from the horrors of Home Rule, and Trenchard."

"Wasn't Trenchard here before?" said Max's mother.

"Yes, five or six years ago. He was with the Royal Scots in Derry. He's high up in the Royal Flying Corps now, I think."

"Don't let Craig hear you calling it Derry, Robert," said Max's mother, and he laughed and squeezed her arm.

"All that UVF nonsense. And now war only days away. If only men realised we're all human beings, the world would be a better place."

"Or if the world was run by women," said Robert.

"Are you turning into a suffragette, mother?" said Max.

"Absolutely. I'd chain myself to this range, if I thought you two would notice the difference."

"Don't worry, mother. At least Fido loves you," said Max.

"Fido loves everyone. Hand me your plate."

Max walked into the kitchen to hear a strange rumble echoing down the corridor from the dining room.

"What on earth is that?" he said.

"Trenchard," said his father. "No wonder they call him Boom. Hard to believe he lost a lung fighting the Boers. Lord help the foundations if he still had both."

"Where's Madam?" said Max.

"I don't know what she's doing," said Mrs Rapier, the cook. "She asked me to get all sorts of strange things down from Omagh, and she's been in the pantry all day."

Max and his father carried the wines through to the drawing room and found the guests already merry on gin and tonics, except for Trenchard, who had just asked for water.

Carson looked stolid, imposing and intelligent, and Craig looked as if he had been born angry, with a face that had apparently been carved with a blunt hatchet.

Trenchard, with his deep eyes, knowing and humorous, and bushy brows and moustache, was somewhat like an earnest spaniel, and Churchill, with his heavy jowls and lips, and wide-set eyes under thinning swept back hair, had the air of a disappointed goldfish.

Kumiko sat among them, like a lily in a gun rack.

"You can bring through the starters now, boy," said the Major. "Apparently Kumiko has a surprise for us."

Kumiko had arranged the delicacies on simple white plates, and as Max removed the linen covers and looked at them, he felt the strangest sensation of peace settling on his soul.

"I say," said his father. "How very pretty."

They picked up the two plates carefully, carried them through to the dining room, and set them down on the dining table.

"What's this muck?" said the Major.

"It is sushi, sir," said Kumiko, stiffening.

"Looks like raw fish and food for rabbits to me. Edwards, is there some mulligatawny left over from last night?"

"Gallons, sir," said Max's father.

"Have it heated. Then bring me some real food. And get rid of this."

Standing across the table from Kumiko, Max saw the brief look of shock and shame that ghosted across her face before she lowered her head.

"I am so sorry, sir. I shall remove it immediately," she said.

"What's on the menu?" said Trenchard.

"Spiced beef. Been marinating in saltpetre for weeks. Vegetables boiled to buggery. Apple crumble, then Stilton. It's been sitting in the pantry since the Boer War, so it's crawling by now. Just the way I like it."

"Didn't you eat this stuff when you were in Japan?" said Carson as Max picked up the sushi plates.

"Good God, no," said the Major. "We had a bloody good officers' mess there. And a bloody good wine cellar. No reason to go native. Max, forget that. Kumiko will do it. Tell Cook to get the soup heated sharpish."

"Isn't it a bit off to call the servants by their first names?" said Churchill.

"I don't make a habit of it," said the Major. "It's just to distinguish him from his father."

"Oh well. Can't be helped. At least he doesn't sound like a Catholic. I assume you don't employ them?" said Craig.

"Can't be helped around these parts, I'm afraid," said the Major.

"Shame. Absolute vermin. Breed like rabbits. Wouldn't have one about the place myself."

"That's a bit harsh, Craig," said Carson.

"Perhaps. I've nothing against them personally, but as a whole they're naturally subversive. If we let them, they'll undo everything we stand for."

"As long as you don't employ homosexuals," said Carson. "The memory of even being in the same courtroom as that mincing pansy Wilde still makes my skin crawl."

"Didn't you know him at Trinity?" said Churchill.

"Vaguely," said Carson.

"Not to mention lesbians. Our late Queen didn't even believe such a thing was possible," said Trenchard, making the glass on the table tinkle.

"Lesbians, homosexuals and Fenians. God preserve us from them all," said Craig.

"Lesbians are homosexuals, sir. The word comes from the Greek for the same, not the Latin for men," said Max before his brain could tell his mouth to stay shut.

"I beg your pardon?" said Craig.

"I said I think it's going to rain later, sir," said Max.

"Don't be smart, boy. Remember your place," said the Major. "Now get that bloody soup organised. Pronto."

"Yes, sir," said Max, and left for the kitchen before he got into any more trouble.

"He's a bit of an upstart for a butler's son," said Craig. "If he worked for me I'd have him thrashed for such impertinence."

"Too smart for his own good. Read every book in the library. Complete waste, since he's just going to be a butler for the rest of his life," said the Major.

"Shame he can't go to grammar school and make something of himself," said Churchill.

"His father did ask me, but I'm afraid if I paid for every bright boy on the estate to get an education, there'd be nobody left to run the estate. No, a butler's son he is, and a butler he will be. Another splash?" said the Major.

"Don't mind if I do. This is excellent," said Churchill.

"Yes, it is quite," said the Major, glancing at the bottle. Châteauneuf-du-Pape. He turned it so that the label faced away from Craig.

"Will you be going to France with the Expeditionary Force, Trenchard?"

"Afraid not. I've been passed over in favour of Henderson and Sykes. Kitchener wants me to stay at home and prepare new squadrons."

"Lucky you. As for me, I'm all at sea," said Churchill, to laughter.

"It is only weeks away? War, I mean," said Craig.

"Days, I fear," said Churchill, and took another sip.

"Well, we have 100,000 good men who signed a solemn league and covenant to fight for God and Ulster, and are now willing to fight for King and Country," said Craig. "All we lack is artillery."

"Artillery's easy," said the Major. "Aim, fire, adjust, repeat."

"You know," said Carson, "if you had asked me a month ago what I saw in the future, I would have said bitter fighting and rivers of blood in the hills and dales of Ulster. But now I fear it will be in the rolling meadows of France and Belgium."

He looked into the fire.

"Quite ironic, though, that the Nationalists may get their united Ireland after all."

"Oh? How so?" said Craig.

"United against the Hun, rather than us, I mean," said Carson.

They were silent, apart from the crackling of the logs in the grate.

"Did you say apple crumble for pudding?" said Churchill.

"Yes. With custard," said the Major.

In the kitchen, Max set down his sushi plate and turned to find Kumiko entering silently with the other one.

"I am so sorry you were embarrassed, Madam," he said.

"You are very kind, Max-san, but it was my own stupid fault," she said, setting her plate down.

"It looks so exquisite. What a waste to throw it out. May I…taste it?"

"Yes, of course. But you should use chopsticks. One moment."

She went to a drawer, took out a roll of silk, and unwrapped it to reveal two ivory chopsticks.

"Now. Like this."

She handed them to him, and their fingers brushed.

"Exquisite, Madam," he said, unsure at that moment whether he meant the infinite delicacy of the food, the touch of her fingers so fleeting it was hardly there at all, or both. "Better than heaven."

"Oh? How so?" she said, amused.

"Because I do not have to die to love it," said Max.

Later, in the pantry, he was clearing up when Cook popped her head around the door with a steaming mug in her hand.

"Max, be a dear and take this up to Nurse. She's feeling a bit poorly, and I thought some hot milk and nutmeg might settle her stomach," she said.

"Nurse is always feeling poorly. Ironic, if you think about it," said Max, taking the mug.

He made his way up the stairs and was walking quietly past the master bedroom when he heard the crash of breaking glass, then the Major shouting.

"It would work properly if you didn't just lie there, damn you! You'll just do have to do that other thing."

There was the sound of a smack, then sobbing. Max tiptoed on, and on the top floor tapped Nurse's door, then took a deep breath and walked in.

She was lying in bed with a copy of *Hard Times*, surrounded by her dozen cats. Max tried not to gag.

"Cook sent this up. Do you want me to open the window and let some air in?" he said.

"Don't be ridiculous. Fresh air's bad for you. Set it down, there's a good boy. Frederick, stop that and use the po under the bed."

Max closed the door, took several deep breaths, then took the back stairs down.

The next day, the Major had organised a shooting party on the moors, and Max was loading for Trenchard, although he may as well not have bothered, since in half an hour, Trenchard had managed only to down one grouse and wing another.

At their feet, Fido sat waiting expectantly, the single kill in a hessian bag beside him.

"Keep your head down, chum, before anyone realises you're neither a pointer nor a setter," whispered Max. Fido looked up with that pained and knowing look he had.

"Oh, for Christ's sake," said Trenchard, as two more birds sailed blithely on. "Knew I shouldn't have had that Bushmills after dinner last night."

"Mind if I have a go, sir?" said Max.

"What? Well, it's…highly irregular, but you may as well. Can't do any worse than me," said Trenchard, handing over his Purdey.

"What a beautiful gun," said Max, caressing the walnut stock.

"A gift from my good friend Lady Dudley," said Trenchard. "Don't drop it."

Up ahead, the beaters trashed, and a pair of snipe rocketed out of the ferns.

Max's gun cracked twice in such close succession that the second shot seemed like an echo of the first, and the birds twitched then sailed to the heath in mirrored arcs, like an ironic reflection of their rise from earth.

"Christ. How did you do that?" boomed Trenchard.

"Don't shoot at them, sir. Shoot where they're going," said Max.

"Yes, I know the theory. I've just never seen it put into practice so…elegantly," said Trenchard, taking back the shotgun as the Major stormed up, his face purple, and slapped Max hard across the face. Stunned, Max fell beside a growling Fido.

"What the blue blazes are you doing, you young pup?" said the Major, raising his hand again.

Trenchard reached out and grasped his arm.

"It wasn't the boy's fault, Martin. I said he could. He's a remarkable shot."

"He may well be, but he's still the son of a butler, and has to remember his place," said the Major, and turned on his heel as Max got to his feet.

"Sorry, boy. I got you into trouble. Didn't mean to," said Trenchard.

"That's all right, sir," said Max, looking bitterly at the retreating back of the Major.

Churchill, Trenchard, Carson and Craig left the next morning after breakfast, and the following evening Max walked into his parents' living room to find his father frowning over the *Belfast Telegraph*.

He looked up as Max came in and hugged his mother.

"We are, it seems, at war with Germany," he said.

Chapter Three

September 1914

"What's going on?" said Max as he rounded the corner of the small yard to find Alan Kilpatrick the estate carpenter and Jim Kilpatrick the sawyer walking towards the big house with several cypress planks over his shoulder.

"Madam wants a new bathroom. As if two isn't enough for fifteen bedrooms," said Alan.

"What's a bathroom?" said Jim, and they laughed, since for anyone outside the big house, a bath was a weekly affair in a tin bath in front of the fire.

"It's not even like a proper bathroom," said Violet, Mrs Rapier's daughter, two days later in the kitchen, after all the hammering and banging had stopped. "Want to see it? I'm taking some towels up for her daily bath. Can you imagine? As if once a week isn't enough."

"Or once a year in Nurse's case," said Cook, and Max laughed, lifted the towels from where they'd been warming over the range, and followed Violet up the stairs.

She opened the door to what had been an ante-room beside the master bedroom, and Max followed her in.

A circular cypress tub fed by two copper pipes for hot and cold water sat on a slate floor, beside a small set of steps and a bench.

A smaller tub sat under two pipes protruding from the white wall, and a paper and cedar lath screen in front of the window cast a diffused light over the scene like a veil.

Violet walked over and dipped her hand in the water to test the temperature.

"Ow. Roasting. She's a strange one. Washes herself all over before she gets in. What's the point of that?"

"It's because the bath is an honourable thing. It's called o-furo," said Max. "So you wouldn't defile it by getting in dirty."

"I never heard the like," said Violet. "Here, give me those towels and I'll tell Madam her bath's ready."

Max walked away down the stairs, trying not to think of Kumiko naked in the room he had just left. He walked back into the kitchen to find Cook reading the previous day's *Belfast Telegraph*.

"It says here some chappie in America has invented an electrical refrigerator to keep food cold," she said.

"Not much need of it here, then," said Max.

"We could always open the door and gather around it in winter to stay warm," said Violet, who had just come back in from upstairs.

The next morning, the Major looked up from his kedgeree at Kumiko.

"Listen, it's about time you stopped wearing those bloody kimonos around the place. Looks bloody stupid. I'll take you up to Belfast tomorrow and get you some decent kit."

Max picked up the coffee pot and shook it, then went to the kitchen to refill it. As he returned, the phone in the hallway gave a preliminary ting, then rang.

"Termon? Yes, I'll get him now. Who may I say is calling?"

He put the phone and earpiece down, and went back to the dining room.

"It's for you, sir. War Office. About the war, I imagine."

The Major gave him a sharp look, then wiped his moustache with a napkin and went into the hall.

"Martin. Yes? What? Today? Yes, of course," they heard him say. The phone clicked, and he came back in.

"I have to go to London. A staff car's calling for me at lunchtime," he said.

"What about Belfast, sir?" said Kumiko.

"What? Oh, for Christ's sake," said the Major, then looked at Max.

"You take the Ghost, boy. You're the only one who can fix the bloody thing, so you may as well drive it. Ever been to Belfast before?"

"No sir."

"I'll give you a map. And a map of Belfast." He disappeared into his study, emerged with two Automobile Association maps and spread them on the dining table.

"Look, here's Robinson and Cleaver. That's where you need to go. Tell them to put it on my account.

"Oh, and now that you've finally stopped growing, we may as well get you your butler's suit, since you'll be wearing it for the rest of your life."

Max hardly slept, then got up at dawn, checked the Rolls-Royce from end to end and top to toe, and had just changed into the white shirt and black trousers he used for helping his father when on duty, when Kumiko appeared from the pantry door and stepped into the small yard.

She was wearing a periwinkle blue kimono with a saffron sash, and carrying a little primrose yellow bag with a silver clasp.

"Ohayō gozaimash, Madam-san. O-genki desu ka?"

"Genki-desu, Max-san," she said, delighted. "And please call me Kumiko. I am not old enough to be a Madam."

"Hai, Kumiko-san," he said, and she laughed, like the chiming of small temple bells.

He opened the door of the Rolls-Royce for her, and she stepped daintily in. He got in the other side, and drank in the smell of leather overlaid with the delicate scent of her.

He could not even begin to name it, but it smelt like the music of her playing the piano, drifting out through the French windows.

It was the first time he had been alone with her, and he could feel his heart trying to escape from his chest like a small bird as he started the engine on the trembler, then switched to magneto.

They trundled down the front lane past the gate lodge to the Bush, then across the railway bridge into Tirooney and past the Nine Mile House which was the old staging post for the Derry to Dublin stagecoach.

As the climbed the Inishatieve hill, the Elliott speedometer slowly crept up to 30, then settled there.

"How did you meet the Major, Kumiko-san?" he said as they passed Ballygawley, both wanting to know and not wanting to know.

"I grew up in Kyoto, the old capital, in a lovely wooden house near the Golden Pavilion," she said.

"One night when I was five, my mother was putting me to bed when she knocked over a candle. In moments, the room was ablaze, and hearing her scream, my father rushed in, picked me up, went to the window and threw me down into the arms of a neighbour who had rushed out on hearing the screams.

"Then he went back in to rescue my mother. That was the last time I saw my parents. I was taken in by an aunt in Tokyo who was a governess for an English family, and she taught me English and music.

"Then I met the Major when he was posted to Tokyo as part of the Anglo-Japanese Alliance and I was appointed as his interpreter.

"He seemed so in command of himself and everyone around him. I suppose I was over-awed. Or perhaps I just missed my father.

"In any case, he was very overwhelming. Then when he heard he was to be posted home, he asked me to marry him."

She paused.

"He promised me a new life," she said, and was about to go on, but then looked out of the window and was silent.

"You know," she said after a while, "sometimes I wake in the night and feel as if I am falling through the air again, watching my father stand there for a moment looking at me, and then turning back into the flames to save my mother. Falling and falling forever."

She paused again, and out of the corner of his eye Max saw her bow her head. He dared not look at her in case she was crying.

"It is the look in his eyes that haunts me. Of infinite love, and longing, and sadness," she said.

"O perhaps it was your look, reflected in his eyes," said Max.

She looked at him.

"Yes, Max. Perhaps it was."

They were silent for a while.

"Tell me about life in Japan, Kumiko-san," he said, and she did for the rest of the journey.

Max, who had never been further than Omagh and had only read about the world beyond in the library in Termon, listened enthralled.

When she had run out of things to say, they sat, serene in each other's company for a while as the Rolls-Royce hummed on, then there was a pop, and he looked over to see her open the clasp on her bag and take out a small book.

"Poems?" he said.

"Haiku. Do you know them?"

"Just Bashô's one about the frog jumping into the pond. And the Irish one."

"The Irish one?"

"Yes.

"Writing a poem
in seventeen syllables
is very diffic."

She looked at him for a second before she understood, then raised her hand to her mouth and burst out laughing.

"Oh Max, that is so funny."

She laughed again, then sighed.

"What a treasure," she said. "What a shame."

Unsure what she meant, or if it was part of another haiku, he was silent as they entered the outskirts of Belfast.

They parked outside Robinson and Cleaver, and were shown in by a doorman in a top hat.

Inside, a tall elegant man sashayed towards them.

"May I help you?" he said to Max.

"Yes, I think we need women's clothing, then men's'," said Max.

"Bespoke or off the peg?"

"What's the difference?" said Max, thinking Pat Rafferty's in Carrickmore was never like this.

"The price and the quality, young sir. Bespoke is made to measure, and off the peg is, well, off the peg."

"Bespoke, then," said Kumiko.

"Perfect," said the man, then looked Kumiko up and down.

"My, that's a lovely combination of colours. Follow me," he said, and swanned ahead of them up a wide marble staircase.

Lucky Carson isn't here, thought Max.

In the gentlemen's bespoke department, a young man about the same age as Max measured every part of him and wrote figures down in a small notebook, and an older man in morning dress spread a variety of black fabrics on a mahogany bench with a brass ruler set into the edge.

"What is this one, please?" said Kumiko, running it through her finger and thumb.

"Wool and cashmere, Madam."

"That will be perfect."

"An excellent choice," said the older man, then turned to Max. "To which side does Sir dress?"

"I beg your pardon?" said Max.

When the side to which Max dressed had been cleared up, he was measured again for a shirt, and Kumiko picked out Egyptian cotton, a black silk tie and a fine pair of black Oxfords.

Then they moved on to the ladies' bespoke department, and Max watched in wonder as Kumiko selected a symphony of silks, linens and cottons, in the colours of the night, of hillside heathers, of the sea and of the sky.

"What do you think, Max-san?" she said as she held a bolt of silk the colour of her eyes around her and gave a flirtatious twirl.

"Exquisite, Kumiko-san."

"This one?"

"All of them," he said, and she laughed.

"Thank you so much, Max, for this day," said Kumiko as they walked back across the small yard in the lilac dusk.

"It was my pleasure, Kumiko," said Max, as she stopped to watch the bats flitting above.

"Sore wa, watashi no kokoro wa utauta," she said, then laughed. "Oh. So sorry. I spoke Japanese."

Yes. It made my heart sing also, thought Max as he watched her disappear into the house.

Kumiko was playing Rachmaninov in the drawing room when the Major appeared in the door of the drawing room, his face puce.

"Kumiko, what is this?" he said icily, brandishing a piece of paper.

She stopped, crossed the room, and took it from him.

"It is the bill from Robinson and Cleaver, sir," she said, bowing slightly.

"Yes, I can see that. This bit." He stabbed the bottom of the sheet with his finger.

"It is for Max's suit, sir."

"Yes. Exactly. Five pounds and ten shillings? For a suit? What in the name of Christ is it made of? Gold leaf? Angel shit? And sixteen shillings for a shirt? Christ Almighty, that's more than his father earns in a week!"

"I thought…you would want him to look smart, sir. I am so sorry if I have offended you," said Kumiko, her eyes cast down to the floor.

"Offended me? Bankrupted me, more like. That boy will be the death of me. Or perhaps you will," said the Major, and stormed out, slamming the door behind him.

Kumiko went back to the piano, and sat there in silence, her hands in her lap.

* * *

Thankfully, the Major was in Omagh a week later when Willie McBride came trotting up the back lane with his horse and cart, on which sat several large boxes from Robinson and Cleaver which had arrived at Carrickmore Station on the train from Belfast.

Max, who was reading Moby-Dick by the window in his parents' living room, looked down to see Kumiko crossing the small yard carrying one, and hurried down to open the door.

"Your suit, Max. I will wait here," she said, handing it to him with a bow.

He took it upstairs to his bedroom, removed the lid and peeled back the tissue paper, then undressed and carefully put on the shirt and suit. He tied the tie, checked it was straight in what reflection he could see between the black spots in the ancient mirror on his dressing table, and walked downstairs.

She looked at him, her face a wonder.

"Perfect," she said.

"They are the most beautiful things I have ever owned," he said, and bowed. "Dōmo arigatō gozaimashita, Kumiko-san."

"Dōitashimashite, Max-san," she said, and bowed back, then turned and walked back to the scullery door.

He watched her go, his heart lost and found and lost again.

Chapter Four

October 1914

Max was in the coach house adjusting the tappets on the Major's Royal Enfield when young Willy Magee, the gardener's son, stuck his tousled head around the door.

"Major wants everyone in the big yard," he said. Max wiped his hands on an oily rag, and got to his feet.

In the yard, he found all the men on the estate gathered around the Major, who stood on the raised platform beside the ornate iron hand pump fed from the well below.

"Men, as you know, we are at war with Germany, although I am assured it will be a short, sharp affair," he said.

"Those of you who have read this week's Tyrone Constitution will also be aware that my good friends Sir Edward Carson and Sir James Craig have rallied the fine young men of the Ulster Volunteer Force.

"Having saved us from Home Rule, they will now save us from the Kaiser as the 36th Ulster Division, and I am asking all of you under thirty to join us in the good fight. The older ones will stay here to keep the home fires burning. And to keep Termon shipshape and Bristol fashion for when we all, God willing, come home to a hero's welcome."

The yard was silent, apart from the distant cawing of the rooks in the Devil's Wood. Every man there knew that being asked by the Major carried somewhat more weight than a polite request.

Then the lone voice of old Tom piped up.

"Sir, may I go as well as young Tom? I missed my chance to fight the Boers because my father needed me at home, God rest him, so this is my last chance to see some action. And get a crack at the Hun."

"Well, Tom, you don't do much over here, so I suppose you can't do any harm over there," said the Major, to laughter.

Tom tried to look hurt, but failed, mostly due to a large grin making full use of his few remaining teeth.

John Jameson stepped forward from where he stood beside his son Adam, and raised a hand the size of a spade

"Sir, may I go as well to look after young Adam?" he said.

"I don't need looking after, Dad," said a pained Adam, to another ripple of laughter from his peers and a dig in the ribs from young Willy Magee.

"Very well, but that is all," said the Major. "Dismissed."

"Please be careful, son. You're very precious to us," said Max's mother, hugging him so hard he thought a rib would break. "I'll kill you if anything happens to you."

"Don't be silly, mother. I'm indestructible," said Max, and kissed her on the cheek, then shook his father's hand.

"Good luck, son. Come back to us," said his father, and before they all burst into tears, Max slung his canvas haversack over his shoulder and walked to the door, then looked down to see Fido at his side, as always.

"Sorry, chum, you're staying put this time," said Max, as his father took hold of Fido and closed the door.

Max walked down the stone stairs to the door with a heart like lead, and emerged into the small yard to find Kumiko standing there, wearing an indigo silk dress with a white lace collar.

"Kumiko-san," he said.

"Max-san. I just wanted to wish you good fortune, and give you something to keep you safe."

She held out a small silk bag the same colour as the kimono she had been wearing that first evening he had seen her by the lake.

Inside, he found a tiny ceramic fish, of midnight blue with gold-edged scales.

"How very beautiful," he said. "How very beautiful."

"A koi carp," she said. "It signifies good fortune, perseverance in adversity, and great strength. In Japan, we revere the carp because of its ability to swim against the current and fluctuating tides."

He looked at her, his heart filled with yearning at the way she almost got fluctuating right, but not quite.

"Thank you so much. I shall treasure it," he said.

"Please come back safe, Max-san," she said, and squeezed his hand.

Chapter Five

November 1914. Finner Camp, Donegal

Dear Mother and Father,

I hope you are well. Compared to Tyrone among the bushes, Donegal is bald and bleak.

There are fourteen of us to a tent, and at least I am in with the Termon lads, but there is nothing to eat but stew, morning, noon and night, and since there is no hot water, we have to clean the dixies out with sods, so that everything is covered in grease, and tastes like it.

Well, except for the water, which tastes of the chloride of lime they put in it. I imagine it's supposed to sterilise it, but all it does is give us the runs.

I'm not sure how bad the war is, but it can't be much worse than the training. They should send the Huns over here, and they'd give up in a week.

Your loving son,
Max

December 1914. Great Northern Hotel, Bundoran

Dear Mother and Father,

The good news is that we are at least out of the tents and into a hotel. And good thing too, since it has been snowing for weeks, and we are still doing endless route marches for no obvious purpose other than to leave us cold and fed up.

The bad news, sadly, is that I am not getting home for Christmas. So much for all the talk of the war being over by now.

I miss you both very much, and Fido. Give him a big snurfle behind the ears for me.

Father, I miss our games of chess as well. I have run out of chaps to play with here, although apparently the rest of the Termon lads have been making a packet betting on me against the officers, so they have promised to buy me a beer at Christmas. I hope that's all right, if it's just one.

Mother, I miss your marrow and ginger jam, so you don't feel left out.

Your loving son,
Max

January 1915. Bundoran

Dearest Mother and Father,

Christmas wasn't so bad in the end, although I did so miss being home with you at Termon.

A special canteen was set up serving currant cake and ginger ale, then in the evening we had a campfire and a sing song, and one of the lads, Private Tom Burrows, entertained us with The Minstrel Boy and I Hear You Calling Me.

He had a very sweet voice, and we all got a bit maudlin, but then John Jameson made us laugh with a rousing chorus of: "And we won't drink chloride of lime! And we won't drink chloride of lime!"

Oh, and John won the 109th Brigade wrestling championships, if you want to tell Margaret and little Annie, since they're always so proud of him. He is a fine chap, as is Adam, although he was as fed up as we all are being stuck here at Christmas.

All the Termon lads are well. Old Tom hasn't been able to do much, so they've given him a yard brush and told him to keep the place neat and tidy, which he does with good heart.

Some of the chaps expected to be in Berlin by now, so are a bit disappointed to have only made it far as Bundoran, although having been no further than Omagh before, I can't tell the difference.

Many thanks for sending me the copies of the *Con*, although they do make me realise how much I miss home. But I've already said that, so I won't go on about it.

I hope you are both well. Say hello to Fido. Or arf, if he prefers.

Your loving son,
Max

PS: I did have that beer, but it wasn't very nice. I felt a bit woozy after, then quite unwell. The lads say I need to practise more.

March 1915. Bundoran

Dearest Mother and Father,

Not much to report, I'm afraid. We had a pep talk last week from a Captain Crozier. Small chubby chap with two chins and a well waxed moustache which he kept stroking lovingly.

"Men," he said, "you must lose your gentle selves. You must steel your hearts and minds and be callous of life and death. That is war."

Since then, we have been losing our gentle selves by sticking bayonets in sandbags filled with straw, and I am now completely callous of life and death, especially towards sandbags.

Your loving son,
Max

May 1915. Seaford, Sussex

Dearest Mother and Father,

What rotten luck. We were posted to Ballycastle and told to prepare ourselves for a grand parade of the entire 36th Division through Belfast, only to be quarantined after several of the lads came down with measles. German ones, I imagine.

Not to be outdone, young Willy Magee and I sneaked out of camp on our day off and got the train to Belfast, where we found a vantage point on a narrow ledge of Robinson and Cleaver's and saw the whole thing. It was the first time I had been there since my day out with Madam Kumiko. Perhaps you would mention it to her and pass on my good wishes, but only if you think it appropriate.

It was, I have to say, a stirring spectacle, and it looked as if the whole city had turned out to see it. Needless to say, we were the envy of the other lads when we got back to camp, and got a proper ragging over it.

As it turned out, we may as well have stayed in Belfast, for the next day we were told to pack our kit, and were taken by train to Great Victoria Street then to Dublin for the Holyhead boat.

Some of the lads were sick on the crossing, but I was all right. We arrived at noon, then for no reason anyone could tell us sat there all night before boarding a train to here.

Still, at least we got bacon and eggs at Crewe. It is absolutely scorching here, and we are all sunburnt.

Your loving son,
Max

October 1915. Bramshott, Hampshire

Dearest Mother and Father,

Apologies for not writing for a while, and even more apologies that this is dashed off in haste.

We were moved to Bramshott for rifle training, since a shortage of ammunition meant that none of us have fired anything for months, but the American bullets were so bad that it I couldn't have hit a barn, never mind the door.

The entire division was reviewed by the King and Kitchener, but sadly I was away dealing with an incident when the musketry instructor got shot. Fortunately, it was only a flesh wound. And it wasn't me, if you're wondering.

Oh, and I saw from the papers a while ago that our old friend Trenchard is now overall head of the RFC. Good for him. He was kind to me when he visited Termon that time, although dreadfully loud.

In any case, we have just been told five minutes ago that we are shipping out to France in the morning, so I had better pack my kit.

At least none of the others will be ill on the crossing, since it is such a still night that all I can hear is the scratching of pens as lads write home to their nearest and dearest.

Which is you, as you know; although don't tell Fido in case he gets upset.

And so, off to war. Wish me luck.

Your loving son,

Max.

He put down his pen, sealed the envelope, then slid his hand into his pocket and touched Kumiko's carp, as he did every morning and every night.

Chapter Six

June 30, 1916. The Somme

Max looked up from cleaning the dirt from under his fingernails with his clasp knife to see a large rat looking at him from the other side of the trench.

"If you're looking for breakfast, you're out of luck," he said. "Maybe Sergeant McMahon will be along in a bit with one of his lardy biscuits. Although if it's any consolation, I can't remember the last time I was fed, watered, warm, clean, dry and vaguely human either."

He pulled down the edge of a puttee and scratched the patch of red, itchy skin caused by the anti-lice powder, then laughed as a louse scuttled out of the puttee, ran across the patch of skin, fell into a puddle beside the duckboard and floated there paddling frantically.

Max fished it out and tapped it onto the wood, and it scuttled off.

"Left right left right. Nicely done, chum. Just watch out for the rat," said Max.

"Here," said young Willy Magee, "do you mind the time Crozier sent us out on patrol and we thought we heard Jerries a couple of yards away, and it was just a rat scraping around inside a beef tin?"

"I do. Another of Crozier's useless patrols. How he made it to Colonel is quite beyond me. Thank God they sent him back to the

107th," said Max as a sloshing sound from down the trench heralded the arrival of Sergeant McMahon in gumboots.

"You're just too late, Sergeant. There was a nice fat rat here a minute ago that would have brightened up lunch no end," said Max.

"How's your feet, lad?" said McMahon.

"Haven't seen them for a while, but your pig fat seems to keep the foot rot at bay. Although I don't think I'll bother washing my socks when I take them off at Christmas," said Max.

"Not a bother, but it works far better inside than outside. Spread it on your biscakes like me," said McMahon, producing a packet of greaseproof paper from his pocket and unwrapping a slab of hard tack lathered in lard.

"Want some?" he said, flicking off a weevil.

"I'll save myself for the smoked salmon at lunchtime," said Max.

"You'll be lucky," said McMahon, taking a bite, wrapping the rest and putting it back in his pocket. "Anyhow, briefing at 1300 hours. Or one o'clock for you simple lads. Or after dinner, if that's even simpler."

"Can't wait," said Willy. "The excitement's killing me."

As McMahon sloshed off, Max heard a rattle of machinegun fire and looked up to see a drab British biplane being pursued by two brightly coloured German aircraft, like a squirrel being tormented by two macaws.

The propeller of the British plane stopped, and it began to spiral down with the green Hun still firing at it.

Max jumped to his feet, raised his rifle and fired, and the green machine leaped, then turned towards the German lines, followed by the yellow one.

"Must have winged him at least," he said, then looked up to where the British pilot was peering over the edge of his cockpit, looking for a meagre flat space in No Man's Land.

He slid down to a narrow stretch, and the plane hesitated, then dropped to the ground. The undercarriage collapsed, then it slid to the edge of a shellhole, teetered there for a moment with the tail in the air, then settled into the mud.

"Nicely done," said Max, then saw four grey-clad figures climb out of the German trenches and start towards the machine.

"Oh no you don't," he said, and raised his rifle to his shoulder again. It cracked, and the first man fell. The others hesitated, then two of them grabbed him under each arm and dragged him back into their trench.

Max climbed out and began to run, slipping and sliding, towards the British machine, from which a thin column of dark smoke was now rising from the engine. He could see the pilot's head moving, and when he was a few yards away, the smoke turned to flame, and the pilot looked at it then turned towards him in despair.

Max got to the cockpit, leaned in and undid the pilot's lap strap, then dragged him free.

He tried to help, then cried out in pain, and Max looked down to where his knee was a tangle of blood and cloth, with a jagged sliver of bone poking through.

"Thank you," said the pilot, looking up, "I —", then fainted.

Max dragged him, slipping and panting, back towards the trench, with bullets cracking and whistling around him, or making a dull phut where they hit the mud around his feet.

No point worrying about them, he thought. It's the one you don't hear that kills you.

At last he made the safety of the trench, and slid down into it, catching his leg on the periscope which was used for viewing No Man's Land, and landing in a heap. The pilot landed heavily on top of him, and he lay there winded as McMahon came sloshing up.

"We'd better get him … to a field dressing station … That knee looks pretty bad," panted Max. "Or maybe … just cover it in pig fat."

"Good work, lad. You'll get a mention in dispatches for that. Or at least an extra biscake," said McMahon, pulling the pilot off Max as the shells began to whistle overhead in the regular morning hate.

Lunch was mouldy potatoes and mildly rancid beef, and as usual, it was stone cold after the long journey from the field kitchens in containers like the ones they used at Termon for bluestone to keep down algae on the lake. Max took a few mouthfuls, then gave the rest to McMahon, who wolfed it down.

At 1 PM, with all the men crammed into the trench and steaming gently in the warm sun after days of rain, Captain Lowry stood on an upturned crate and held up his hand.

Lowry was one of the few officers the men had time for. Although he had been a law student and a member of the OTC at Queen's before the war, there were no airs and graces about him, and Max had additional reason to respect him because Lowry had beaten him at chess.

"Men, as you will have gathered from the barrage over the past week, there is a very big push on, and the 36th is to play our part in it."

"Is this the big push to gain the few yards we lost the last time, or the big push to lose the few yards we gained the time before?" muttered Max.

"Don't be cheeky, lad," growled McMahon.

"He can't help it, sir. He was born that way," said young Willy Magee.

Of the twenty men who had come out from Termon, Max and Willy were the only ones left fighting.

Old Tom had been judged unfit for battle and placed on permanent sentry duty, and young Tom had been one of the lucky ones, with a bullet in the knee which was not bad enough to kill him, but good enough to get him sent home to Blighty.

Of the ones who had died, it was hard to tell which had been the worst.

Jim Kilpatrick the sawyer, who'd saved all their lives one night when they were sitting eating bully beef and hard tack.

Suddenly he'd sniffed the air, jumped up, pulled out his knife, and started hammering on the shell case they'd hung up for warnings.

"Gas!" he'd shouted. "Gas!"

"Don't be daft. It's just the smell from the disinfectant in the latrines," said Willy, but the rest of them were already fumbling for their gas masks.

At least you could smell the chlorine gas. It was the phosgene that had got Jim, with its faint whiff of mouldy hay which was almost impossible to distinguish from the damp smell of men and clothes who were sodden morning, noon and night.

They'd thought he was all right at first, then after two days he started coughing up pint after pint of yellow fluid. It had taken him another two days of agonizing retching to drown in it.

Or John Jameson, who had been crawling ahead of them cutting barbed wire on another of Crozier's useless patrols when a German bullet hit the phosphorus grenade he was carrying in his webbing pouch.

Ablaze and entangled in the wire, he had screamed for someone to shoot him, but as a horrified Max raised his rifle, there was a crack beside him and he looked to see Adam Jameson standing there lowering his gun.

Max would never forget the expression on his face.

Pinned down by German fire, they hid there in the sunken Thiepval to Hamel road as his father burned for half an hour, and the stench of roasted flesh hung in the air all night until a downpour washed some of it away and gave them enough cover to sneak back to their trenches.

Adam disappeared later that morning. He was picked up by the military police on the coast two weeks later, having abandoned his uniform, weapon and equipment.

They brought him back, let him write a letter home to his mother Margaret and pray with the chaplain. Then they got him very drunk, tied him to a stake in the back garden of a villa at Mailly-Maillet, and shot him in front of the entire battalion.

No one carried a phosphorus grenade in their webbing pouch after that.

Max shook his head to clear the memory, and looked up to where Lowry was pointing with his swagger stick at a map which had been pinned to a trench support.

"Right, pay attention. We are here. Jerry is here, here and here. The key objective of the 36th is to capture here, the Schwaben Redoubt.

"Now, I know it's a bit of a hike up to it, giving the Huns the advantage of height, and we have counted sixteen rows of wire guarding the first line of trenches, and five guarding the second.

"However, as you've undoubtedly noticed over the past week, we have flung 1.7 million shells at the Hun trenches, so apologies if it's disturbed your slumbers, but it hopefully means that all we'll find on the other side of No Man's Land are shattered trenches. And maybe a nice farewell note from Hans and Co.

"As well as that, when we attack tomorrow morning, a creeping barrage will move ahead of you to mop up any remaining Huns.

"Once we take the Redoubt, we can stop for lunch, and then I'm reliably informed it's open country all the way to Berlin."

He paused for a laugh, which never came.

"Yes, well. Sergeant Malone will now read out the list of kit you're to carry tomorrow. Don't worry if you don't remember it all. It'll be passed around this afternoon. Malone?"

Malone stepped up on the crate, held a piece of paper stiffly in front of him, cleared his throat and began to read.

"Packs and greatcoats are not to be carried. Haversacks will be worn on the back, containing shaving and washing kit, one pair socks, iron rations and rations for Z Day.

"A waterproof sheet with cardigan inside will be rolled on the back of your belt. Make sure it's no wider than your pack so it doesn't catch on the wire."

"Cardigans? What do we need cardigans for?" said Willy.

"In case we catch a chill. Or get invited to afternoon tea," whispered Max.

"Quiet!" hissed McMahon.

"Every man will carry two bombs, one in each side pocket, two sandbags tucked into his belt and 170 rounds of SAA ammunition," Malone went on.

"Every man of the second and third platoons will carry a pick or shovel. Sergeant McMahon will distribute these, as well as wire cutters.

"Each man with a wire cutter will be issued with a white tape, to be tied around his left shoulder strap, and each company will carry five flags for indicating the position of the most advanced infantry."

He finished, and Lowry took his place on the crate.

"Thank you, Sergeant. That's all, gentlemen. Zero hour will be 0730, and the barrage will move ahead of you in a series of steps at 0733, 0748, 0758, 0848 and then at 1008 to an area 300 yards past the final German line, which you will have captured by then. I won't bore you with the details, but I'm sure it will all go like clockwork."

He paused, and looked around them all.

"Tomorrow will hopefully be a great day for the 36th, so try to get some kip tonight. Good luck to you all."

As he stepped down off the crate, he glanced over, saw Max and pushed his way through the throng.

"Hello, Edwards. Ready to die for King and Country?" he said with an ironic smile.

"Ready to live for Tyrone, sir," said Max, and Lowry laughed.

"We'll have another game tomorrow night. About time I beat you again."

"It was only the once, sir," said Max, and Lowry slapped him on the back.

"It was. But it was a good once."

He paused, and looked through the periscope at No Man's Land.

"You know," he said, "I've just come from the briefing at Divisional HQ, and the Somme Valley is the picture of bucolic bliss. The farmers are out making hay, the air is sweet with elderflower and the mustard seed has turned the whole valley into the fields of Cloth of Gold, with clumps of red clover here and there. Quite beautiful."

"Sir, may I ask a question?"

"Of course."

"Do you think it's wise carrying all that kit tomorrow? It's going to make progress very slow."

"Ours not to reason why, Edwards. And besides, we don't want to waste time coming back for it, now, do we? Anyway, see you for that game tomorrow night. A shilling says it's mine," said Lowry, tapping Max briskly on the arm with his swagger stick and making his way back through the steaming throng.

In that moment, thought Max, they looked like cattle at Omagh Mart.

The sun sank in a blaze of glory, and in the freezing dark, Max leaned against the spade McMahon had given him and looked up at the star shells bursting in many colours above the trenches. So very beautiful, he thought, pulling a blanket around him and trying in vain to sleep.

From the reserve trenches, the sound of men singing "Abide with Me" drifted up on the wind.

Then the wind changed, and he couldn't hear it. And then the barrage started, and he couldn't hear anything except for the howl and whistle of the shells overhead on their way to the German trenches, like all the lost souls of the world returning to Hades.

It stopped for while in the hollow of the night, and in the thundering silence, Max heard the call of a bird.

"Is that a nightingale?" he said, and Willy cocked an ear.

"Water hen, I think," he said, as the barrage began again.

"You asleep, Willy?" he said at four in the morning, the lowest ebb.

"No chance. I'm afraid, and I'm tired, and I want to go home."

"Good idea. Who would you see about that?" said Max, and Willy gave a sardonic snort as above their heads the grey light of dawn slowly turned to the blue sky of a glorious day.

He slept for a while, and dreamed he was back at Termon, walking in the Glen with Fido, then woke with a start as the barrage started again.

He looked at his watch. It was 6.25 AM.

"Surely nothing can live through that," said Willy as the shells thundered overhead on their way to the German trenches.

"Let's hope not," said Max, as McMahon appeared with a flagon of rum.

"No thanks," said Max.

"I'll have yours, then," said Willy.

"Scouts have just come back. Doesn't look like the barrage has done much damage to the wire," said McMahon.

"Jesus," said Willy.

Above their heads, impossibly, the howl of shells got worse. Then stopped. The seconds became minutes, and at 7.30, whistles began to blow all along the line and it started again.

"Have you packed your cardie? Just in case you catch your death," said Willy, as they clambered up over the firestep.

All around them, hundreds of men walked forward as slowly and earnestly as if they were on a route march back at Finner.

They had only gone a few yards when the Spandaus started, and instantly the air became a hell of whistling bullets.

Men began to fall, at first one at a time, then in their dozens.

They trudged and stumbled on, with the shells screaming above, men screaming all around, and in between the deathly rattle of machinegun fire. The very air seemed hot with hissing metal, and the earth rocked as shells crashed down ahead of them.

"Bloody artillery. Aren't they supposed to be ranging ahead of us?" said Willy.

To their left, McMahon clutched his chest, gave a strange cough, then slipped on the mud and fell into a flooded shellhole, borne down by the weight of all the gear he was carrying. They heard him screaming, then a gurgling and thrashing, then nothing.

Max struggled out of his pack, slid down after him and was immediately submerged in the muddy water. Somehow he found a foothold on something solid, and got his head above the surface, choking and spluttering.

Taking a deep breath, he plunged under again and hunted around with his hands until his fingers snagged on McMahon's webbing.

He hauled him clear of the surface, but the only light in his unblinking eyes was the reflection of the blue sky and white puffy clouds above.

"I'll come back for you, Sarge," said Max, then let him slide below the surface and looked up to see Willie peering over the edge of the shellhole.

Max grabbed the proffered hand, hauled himself out, and stuck his spade in the mud.

"You can't leave that," said Willy as they trudged on, side by side.

"To hell with it. I'll come back for it later. Besides, it'll show us where the Sergeant is," said Max.

Lowry was a few yards ahead of them, strolling as if he was on a Sunday outing, when a shell took his head off. He walked on for a yard, still clutching his swagger stick, then folded elegantly to the ground.

They walked past his body, and met a Corporal wandering the other way carrying his own arm with a white tape still tied around the top, and the fingers at the other end clutching a pair of wire cutters.

"Kevin, I'm looking for Kevin. Have you seen Kevin?" he said, then collapsed.

"Somebody must have seen Kevin," he said, and died.

Max prised the wire cutters from his fingers, and cleared a path through the row of wire ahead. He and Willy crawled through, then ducked as a machinegun nest homed in on them from the German trenches.

They piled a couple of bodies up as shelter and hid behind them, one with no legs and the other with the top of his head missing.

"We're stuck here, and they're too far to get with a grenade," said Max.

Willy glanced around the mess of skull and brains he was hiding behind, then ducked back again.

"Not a bit of it," he said, then unclipped a Mills bomb from his webbing strap, pulled the pin and in one swift movement rose to his knees, threw and was down again.

There was a crump, and the Spandau fell silent.

"Good man," said Max. "I knew those cricket ball throwing skills would come in handy some day."

"And not even a greenhouse to worry about," said Willy, and they were up and running, slipping and sliding, towards the German trench.

As they reached it, a handful of grey figures swarmed out like starving wolves. Max downed one, then another was almost on top of him.

Without thinking, he plunged his bayonet into the man's stomach, and the German sank to his knees, his hands clutching the scabbard as he looked down in disbelief.

Then he looked up at Max, his eyes filled with longing before they closed.

"Christ, this is awful," said Max, then looked down to a warren of trenches spiralling down further than the eye could see.

"Bloody hell, so that's how they did it," said Willy beside him. "Millions of shells to dig a bunch of holes, and all they did was just dig deeper ones."

Max turned to see a dozen more men coming up behind them, led by a Corporal.

"Patterson," he said, holding out a hand covered in mud and blood. "You the 36th?"

"Yes," said Max.

"Which Brigade?"

"109th. You?"

"107th."

"How many of you are left?"

"This is it. From our company, at any rate."

"Jesus God," said Willy.

"Any ammunition left?" said Patterson.

"A dozen clips between us. You?"

"Aye, same, more or less," said Patterson, then looked at Max. "Do you know your face is a funny shade of yellow?"

"So is yours. Must be jaundice."

"Cordite and lidite, more like. From all those nasty explosions," said Willy.

They waited until nightfall, by which time it was obvious no reinforcements were coming.

From the next line of enemy trenches, an occasional rattle of Spandau fire kept their heads down, and on either side, they could see shadowy grey figures flitting in the dark.

"Looks like we're the only ones who've got this far," said Max.

"Which means we're surrounded on three sides," said Willy. "If that makes sense."

"This is suicidal," said Patterson. "Jerry will be all over us in a minute. I think we should regroup under cover of darkness and find out what's happening."

"I hate to go back, but it makes sense to me," said Max.

"You know, I'm getting rightly scundered with this," said Willy above another Spandau rattle.

It stopped, and he glanced over the edge of the trench, then turned to Max.

"When we get home to Termon, I —"

He stopped, and a bloody hole flowered where his left eye had been. The other one looked on at Max for a moment, then past his shoulder into the lost future, and then young Willy Magee's head slumped against Max's shoulder, as if he was just resting there.

Max put his arm around him and held him, until his body had grown as cold as the starry sky above them.

"Come on, let's go back. I'll carry him," he said. Patterson helped him lift the body of Willy over his shoulder, and they started to make their way back from the gates of hell.

All around them as they made their way, men groaned, screamed or called hopelessly out for some solace from God, their mothers, or both.

They got back to where Max had left his spade, and he was stooping to retrieve it when everything went black.

As they say, it’s the bullet you don’t hear that gets you.

Chapter Seven

July 3, 1916

Max opened his eyes to find a pair of large brown ones looking back at him with a concerned expression. Above them, a starched white hat was struggling to contain a tumbling mass of nut-brown curls, and below them, a pale face tapered elegantly to a gently pointed chin.

"Bonjour," he said.

"Pardon?"

"Bonjour?"

"Ah, bonjour," she laughed, correcting his pronunciation.

"Oh. Sorry. I learned it from a book, and there was no guide to how to say it."

"That's all right. I speak English anyway."

"Where am I?"

"Number 84 General Base Hospital. Near Maranique. Mostly flying fellows."

"What happened?"

"You were lucky. A fractured skull, but if that bullet had been an inch to the left, you would be in the morgue rather than looking at me."

"Lucky me, then. Max Edwards. Private, Second Class." He held out his hand.

"Yvette Leroy-Beaulieu. First class nurse." Her hand was cool and firm.

“Delighted,” said Max.

Max was sitting up in bed reading *The Illustrated London News* when the water glass on the bedside table began to tremble, and a booming sound echoed down the corridor.

“That sounds familiar,” he said, as the doors swung open to reveal Matron and a doctor leading in the imposing figure of Trenchard followed by another officer with a thin, slightly strained face and a wispy moustache.

He made his way down the ward chatting to the RFC men in each bed, then was walking past Max’s bed when he turned back and looked.

“Aren’t you young Edwards from Termon?” he said.

“I am, sir,” said Max. “Good to see you again.”

“The Oxford marmalade was bloody good there. What have you done to yourself?”

“Head wound. No vital organs involved. Apparently a Hun bullet left a nice groove in my skull. I can use it to keep my pencil.”

Trenchard laughed.

“Where are you being posted when you get out of here?”

“Back to the Poor Bloody Infantry, I imagine. Not that there’s much left of the 36th after the Somme.”

Trenchard looked at him.

“Nonsense. We need crack shots like you in the air, not up to their neck in mud. Especially after Bloody April. Take a note, Baring,” he said to his aide-de-camp, and swept on, then paused and turned back to Max.

“Oh, you might like to know that our mutual friend Major Martin has been transferred to Artillery.”

“Thank you, sir,” said Max, who could have cared less, but not very much.

As Trenchard and entourage left the ward, the RFC man in the next bed began to laugh.

“What’s so funny?” said Max.

“Take a note, Baring. It’s been a catchphrase in the squadron for ages, but I hadn’t a clue where it came from until now.”

Chapter Eight

August 1916. Central Flying School, Upavon Aerodrome, Wiltshire

Max climbed out of the Crossley tender, shouldered his kitbag and stood on the grass in front of a long, low wooden building with a balcony along the front and the word OFFICES painted above.

A door opened, and an officer walked up to him. Max stood and saluted.

"Are you Edwards?"

"Yes sir."

"I'm Captain Babington. Leave your bag here. This way."

He led Max into the building and down a corridor, then knocked on a door.

"Come," said a voice, and they walked in to find a man in a Royal Navy uniform sitting behind a desk writing. His white cap hung from a coat stand in the corner, and he stopped writing and looked up to reveal a face which somehow managed to be stern, kindly and sad at the same time.

"Edwards, sir."

"Ah yes. Trenchard mentioned you. I'm Captain Paine. Babington, fetch Sanderson, will you? Edwards, take a seat."

Two minutes later, a slightly faded man in his late thirties walked in, removed the pipe from his mouth and saluted Captain Paine.

"Ah, Sanderson. This is your latest Hun. Trenchard thinks highly of him, so God knows what that means."

"Hun, sir?" said Max.

"Because you're more dangerous to us than the enemy. At least until Sanderson teaches you to land without killing yourself," said Paine.

"Funny enough, Trenchard was here back in 1912," said Sanderson as Max collected his bag and they walked away across the grass.

"Was he a good pilot?"

"Dreadful. Thank God Copland Perry taught him, not me. How he got his ticket in an hour and four minutes was quite beyond both of us. And thank God they promoted him to flying a desk," said Sanderson.

"My father said he lost a lung in the Boer War."

"He did, and was partially paralysed to boot. Took up bobsleighing, of all things, then crashed on the Cresta Run and miraculously clicked his spine back into place. Remarkable chap. Stubborn as an ox."

He paused.

"Still an awful pilot, though. Bloody's a much better natural flyer."

"Bloody, sir?"

"Captain Paine. The CO. Although don't ever call him that."

"Of course. Have you been out there, sir?" said Max.

"Afraid not. Dodgy ticker," said Sanderson, tapping his chest with his pipe, "although why they think that students trying to kill me every day is any less stressful than Huns doing the same thing is quite beyond me."

He paused, and they looked around at the rising note of an aircraft engine in distress.

They were just in time to see a large biplane which was taking off collide with another one which was coming in to land. There was a sickening, rending crash of splintering wood and ripping fabric, and the two fell to the grass in a fatal embrace.

"Oh dear," said Sanderson. "Third one this week. I'm fed up telling chaps to keep a good lookout in the circuit.

"Do you ride, by the way?"

"I probably would, if I had a horse, sir. Why do you ask?"

"We like chaps who ride, play sport, that sort of thing. If you can control a horse, you can usually control an aeroplane. Still, never mind. We'll just see how you get on."

They had reached a wooden cabin, and Sanderson knocked and went straight in. Max followed him, to find a wood-burning stove in the middle and two lockers with a camp bed beside each one.

On one of them lay a handsome young man with curly russet hair, a rosy, cheerful expression and a strong chin, with one hand behind his head and the other clutching a copy of *Punch*.

"Priory, this is Edwards. He'll be sharing with you," said Sanderson.

"Right-o," said Priory. "Listen, this cartoon is very clever. The captain says to the girl: 'Your brother is doing splendidly in the Battalion. Before long he'll be our best man'. And she says: 'Oh Reginald! Really, this is so very sudden'."

"Yes, very good," said Sanderson. "Edwards, get yourself settled in. I'll see you at 8 AM for your first lesson. I hope to Christ you're better at landing than Priory."

"That's very cruel, sir. I'm deeply hurt," said Priory.

"You'll get over it," said Sanderson as an elderly man in uniform walked in.

"Symes, this is Edwards," said Priory.

"Good afternoon, Mr Edwards. I am the batman for you young gentlemen," said Symes. "Let me know if there is anything you need."

He bowed slightly, then left with Sanderson.

"Good heavens. Wait till my father hears I have a servant. Or half a one," said Max.

"Why, what does your old man do?" said Priory.

"He's a butler. What's yours?"

"Barrister. Same thing as yours, then. Begins with b, and wears the same kit to work every day."

Max decided that he liked Priory.

"What's flying like?" he said, as he dumped his kit on the camp bed.

"Oh, flying's easy, sport. Landing's the tricky bit. As Sanderson so kindly pointed out. I only cracked it when I realised that the secret is just to look at yon far distant hedge and keep the bloody thing flying down the field until it lands itself. Works most of the time. Before that, I just used to throw it at the grass and hope for the best.

"Oh, and another piece of advice: don't get too slow then stick in a bootful of rudder, or you'll end up in a spin. Especially close to the ground. I've seen several chaps go that way."

"Ah yes, I overheard someone else talking about that on the way up. Didn't some Navy chap called Parke work out how to get out of it a few years ago?

"So he said. Then he crashed and killed himself four months later. I rest my case, your worship."

"By the way, doesn't anyone have first names around here?" said Max.

"Chaps don't need first names, so they become rusty through lack of use. Then they're sold to scrap yards and sent to our colonial friends in America in return for last names they don't use. A very amicable agreement, but if you wish to break centuries of tradition, I'm Bentley."

"Max," said Max, shaking his hand. "That's a strange name."

"Quite. Pater and mater named me after the old house of the same name down in Middlesex. They used to take the train down from Harrow, and apparently I was conceived in the bluebell wood in the grounds. Lovely old place. Designed by Soane in 1775."

He looked at his watch, then sat bolt upright.

"Bloody hell, didn't realise the time. I was supposed to meet Angela five minutes ago."

"Is she your girlfriend?"

"Good God, no. Barmaid at the Ship Inn," said Bentley, and throwing his jacket over his shoulder, dashed out the door.

* * *

The next morning, Max clumped across the grass wearing a heavy, hair-lined leather coat two sizes too big. In one hand he carried a fur-lined leather flying helmet, and in the other a pair of goggles and a pair of huge gauntlets made of some strange kind of scratchy yellowish hair.

Captain Sanderson was standing beside a biplane which looked both frail and imposing. At the front of it stood a corporal, looking vaguely bored and holding a large brass syringe. Another stood by the tail, looking equally bored.

"Morning, Edwards. Ready to fly?" said Sanderson.

"I think so, sir. Will we be able to take off with all this clobber?"

"I imagine so," laughed Sanderson, then turned to the aircraft. "Welcome to the Avro 504. Get into the back seat, and I'll talk you through the controls and the instruments."

"Get in? How?"

"Just put your left foot in that hole, then swing your right foot in. You can hold onto the leather rim of the cockpit, but nothing else. Then put your feet on the seat, grab the rim with both hands, and slide yourself down. You can put your feet on the metal panels on either side, but not on the wires or the fabric."

Max did as he said, feeling spectacularly clumsy.

"Right, now do up your lap strap," said Sanderson.

Max looked down, then all around the cockpit.

"Er, where is it, sir?" he said helplessly.

Sanderson peered into the cockpit, then laughed.

"You're sitting on it, you mug. Lift up. Right, instruments."

Max looked at the five dials and what looked like an upside down smile on the wooden panel in front of him as Sanderson explained each one.

"At this stage you can forget about most of them except the airspeed indicator on the left there. You must keep that above 43 mph, or we fall out of the sky and die. Got that?"

"Yes, sir."

"Good. Now, see this switch on top of the stick? That's the blip switch. You'll hear me using it to blip the engine, since rotary engines are complete pigs. They only have two speeds, flat out and death to pilots, and this keeps it in a nice happy place somewhere in the middle. Anyway, you'll see when we get airborne. Happy enough?"

Hysterical, thought Max.

"Er, yes, I think so. Sir," he said.

"It's a bit noisy when we get up there, and you may not be able to hear what I say, but once we're in the air, I'll demonstrate straight and level flight and a few turns, and you just keep your hands on the stick and your feet on the rudder bar and follow through, then you can have a go on your own. Got all that?"

"I think so, sir."

"Good," said Sanderson, then climbed into the front cockpit with practised ease, buckled himself in and looked up to the corporal at the front.

"Ready!"

The corporal turned the propeller and squirted something into each cylinder with the syringe.

"Switch off, sir!"

"Switch off. Suck in."

The corporal turned the propeller three times.

"Switch on, sir!"

Max saw Sanderson reach down to the left of the cockpit.

"Switch on."

The corporal reached up to his full height, gave the propeller a mighty swing, and the engine burst into life with a fearsome rattle. The whole machine shook as if alive.

"Chocks away!" shouted Sanderson, blipping the engine and waving his hand to and fro, and the corporal dashed around the spinning propeller and busied himself under the aircraft.

It began to lumber across the grass, and remembering what Sanderson had said, Max rested his right hand lightly on the wooden stick and his feet on the rudder bar, and felt Sanderson feeding in right rudder and easing the stick forward gently.

The tail came up, and he could now see the far hedge over the nose, and then he felt Sanderson easing the stick back, and before he knew it, the bouncing and vibration had stopped, and the grass below them was falling away as the Avro rose into its natural element.

"Gosh," said Max.

The altimeter slowly crept up until it read 1000 ft, and Sanderson shouted back: "Right, now look over the nose. This is straight and level flight. You have control, so keep it steady at that."

After half a minute, Sanderson declared himself satisfied.

"Good. Try to relax and be gentle, and don't over-correct so much. Now a turn to the right. Follow through, then it's your turn. Remember to use the rudder as well as the stick in the turn to avoid adverse yaw."

"Adverse what?" said Max, but his query was swept away on the wind.

They did gentle then steeper turns, then climbing and descending for half an hour until Max had mastered the knack of juggling the block tube, fine adjustment levers and blip switch which controlled the engine.

"Excellent," shouted Sanderson. "Right, that's quite enough for the moment. We'll head back, have a cup of tea, then try some takeoffs and landings. I have control."

I'm glad you do, thought Max, looking over the side as Sanderson swung the plane around, since I haven't a flipping clue where we are, or where the aerodrome is.

He was still looking over the side when there was a frightful roar, and another Avro swept overhead what seemed like only inches away. Max jumped, then ducked and looked up just in time to see Bentley peering down with a grin.

"Good grief," said Max. "I don't know about you, sir, but he scared the heck out of me. Sir?"

In front of him, Sanderson's head lolled to the left, and the plane slowly began to spiral down as if following his lead.

"Oh God," said Max. "His dodgy ticker."

He grabbed the stick, and brought the plane back to straight and level. Right, right, calm down. Compass. We'd been heading 090.

He banked into a turn, and the compass swung crazily, then finally settled. No, wrong. The other way. Of course. They'd been banking to the left, so he needed to go right. That was better. Now where the hell was the aerodrome?

He looked around, and saw nothing he recognised. Hardly surprising, since he'd been concentrating so hard on flying. Wait. The village, and the squat grey church tower. There it was, and the aerodrome was past that. But in which direction?

Think, Max! When he'd passed through it in the tender, he'd had to shield his eyes from the sun on the road to the aerodrome, so it must be…yes! His eyes caught the glint of sunlight on the wings of a banking aircraft, and he saw the field, with the hangars to one side, the road and the huts on the other side.

As he breathed a sigh of relief, the stick started to become mushy in his hand, and he became conscious of a thrumming over the wings. What, what? Airspeed! He glanced down, and saw to his horror that he'd been pulling back on the stick, and the airspeed was dropping through 45 mph.

He pushed the stick forward, and the Avro began to fly again, then looked back at where the aircraft he had spotted was on its final approach to land.

"That gives me the direction, at any rate," he said, then, keeping a careful eye on the airfield so as not to lose it again, flew a couple of miles past it then turned carefully to land in the same direction as the previous aircraft.

"Right, here goes," he muttered. "Just relax and be gentle, as Sanderson said."

He pointed the plane down at the field, then realised from the whistle of the wind in the wires that he was gaining speed. He glanced at the airspeed indicator, and saw to his horror that it registered seventy.

Blip, blip, flipping blip. He pressed the blip switch on and off, and the whistling died down.

The field grew closer, and he passed over the hedge too high and too fast. What was it Bentley had said? Look at the far hedge and keep the machine flying until it landed itself.

He eased the stick back and kept looking at the hedge as the Avro sank. The thrumming started again. It was too late to do anything about it now. He held his breath, willing it to keep flying, and it bounced once, twice then settled on the grass and the nose came up as the tail sank.

He relaxed and breathed for the first time in an eternity, but in doing so let his thumb slip off the blip switch.

The engine bellowed like an angry bull, and the Avro accelerated out of control towards a hangar.

"Stop, stop!" he cried. How did you make the bloody thing stop? He pressed the blip switch again, but the hangar grew larger and larger.

Then he remembered: Sanderson had reached down to his left to switch something on before the corporal had swung the prop.

Where? Where? All he could see was something that looked like a brass light switch. He flicked it down, the engine stopped, and the plane came to a halt two yards from the hangar.

In the sudden silence, all he could hear was his breathing and the blood thundering in his ears, and he suddenly realised he was soaked in sweat.

He looked around him, hardly able to believe that he was safely back on the ground, and saw the CO walking over.

"Nice enough landing, Edwards. I expect Sanderson will be sending you solo after that."

"I'm afraid I don't think Sanderson will be doing anything, sir. He seems to be slightly dead," said Max.

"Good grief," said Paine, looking into the front cockpit. "Poor old Sanders."

They pulled Sanderson out and laid him down. He looked quite peaceful, for someone who had just been frightened to death.

"Go and get a couple of stretcher bearers, if you would," said the CO.

As Max was walking towards the medical tent, he met Bentley coming the other way.

"Whoops," said Bentley.

"Whoops is right," said Max. "Lucky you gave me that tip about landing."

They found a stretcher, and bore Sanderson to the medical tent. With nothing more to do, they lay down in the sun, and Max was suddenly aware of the sweet smell of the freshly cut grass, and of the infinite attraction of life.

The next morning, he clumped across the grass to find Babington standing beside the Avro.

"Circuits and bumps today, Edwards. Do try not to kill me as well, will you?" said Babington. "We only have a limited supply of instructors, you know."

"I'll do my best, sir. I mean not to," said Max, and climbed in.

They spent half an hour taking off, flying around and landing again, then Babington got out.

"Right, off you go on your own," he shouted from beside the cockpit. "Since you've already done this, there's not much I can tell you, but you're still inclined to land a bit fast, so watch that. Just keep holding off until the aircraft lands as slowly as possible. Oh, and be aware that without me on board, she'll handle a lot lighter and climb a lot faster."

"Cripes, he wasn't kidding," said Max, as the Avro left the ground before he knew it and leaped skywards like an angel who was late for tea. He was at circuit height in what seemed like half the time, then curved around, enjoying the feel of the more responsive craft, got everything nice and steady on the downwind leg, then slid round and down over the hedge, easing gently back on the stick and settling down to a nice three-pointer.

He cut the engine in front of the hangar he had nearly destroyed the day before, and Babington walked over, reached up and shook his hand.

"Congratulations, young man," he said. "I do believe you are a pilot."

"Gosh," said Max. "Thank you, sir."

* * *

"Right," said Babington, "now that we have somehow taught you gentlemen to fly, we are somehow going to teach you how to shoot things down. This is Sergeant Cooper, who will be your musketry instructor. Delightful term. You will start today on basic rifle craft with the .303 Lee Enfield, then move on to the Lewis gun and Vickers machine guns. Sergeant, they're all yours."

They marched in pairs to the firing range with a Private called Barkley, and Cooper talked them through the rifle and the safety procedures.

"Right, gentleman, you will see a row of targets 100 yards away. If you cannot see the targets, raise your hand and I will get you posted to the PBI," he said, to a ripple of laughter.

"Already been there, sir," said Max. "I wouldn't recommend it."

"Ah yes, so I heard. Right, let us commence firing. You have ten rounds. Let's see who can put the most in the target."

When they had finished their clip, Barkley stood by with a clipboard, and Cooper raised his binoculars.

"Right, Barkley, stand by. Priory, ten on target. Well done, Priory. Odell, seven, Wilcox six, Hughes seven, Ferrie six, Alcock five. Tut tut, Alcock. Edwards…one. Dearie, dearie me, Edwards. Perhaps you should have stuck with the PBI after all."

"One, sir? I bet you a pint it's not," said Max.

"A pint? You're on, you impertinent whippersnapper. Come with me. Barkley, hold these."

He handed his binoculars to Barkley, and marched to the target with Max, then bent over and peered at it. In the centre was a ragged hole the size of a beer mat into which Max had poured all ten rounds.

"Good grief," said Cooper. "I take it back. Thank Christ you're on our side."

"I'm going to enjoy that pint, sir."

"Cheeky bastard," said Cooper. "Why on earth didn't they mark you out for a sniper at Aldershot?"

"The American ammunition was so poor you couldn't hit a barn door with it, sir. And besides, things got a bit confused after Wallace shot the musketry sergeant."

"Good God. Deliberately?"

"I think it was an accident, sir. Although with Wallace's shooting, it was difficult to tell."

September 1916

"Pigeons," said Babington.

"Pigeons, sir?" said Max, looking up from his copy of *The Times*.

"Yes, pigeons. Our observation chaps in France have been having a spot of bother with these new Marconi radios for reporting back to Artillery, so they want us to find some way of releasing homing pigeons from aircraft as a back-up."

"Why not just throw the little buggers out and let them fly back?" said Bentley.

"Because the wash from the propeller divests the poor little buggers of most of their feathers, Priory, leaving them to plummet to earth with a muffled squawk."

"Oh dear."

"We've tried everything. We even made them little harnesses and tied them together with six-foot cords, then released them from cages attached to the bomb racks to keep them out of the prop wash. The theory was that they'd fly against each other and descend gracefully to earth," said Babington.

"Did it work?"

"Not exactly. They panicked, got themselves in a tangle, and plummeted to earth in a harmony of muffled squawks. Then we tried little parachutes. That didn't work either."

"Oh well. If God had wanted pigeons to fly, he would have sent them to Upavon," said Bentley.

"Thank you, Priory. Very helpful, as always," said Babington.

"Glad to be of service, sir," said Bentley.

"Mmm," said Max.

That evening, they were sitting on the communal latrines when Max looked at the toilet roll.

"You know what? I've just had an idea," he said.

"What, you mean wrap them in toilet roll and toss them out of the cockpit?" said Babington the next day.

"It'll keep their feathers in place, sir. Then as they fall, the paper will unwrap and they'll just fly away," said Max.

"Mmm. Well, it's worth a try, I suppose," said Babington, then turned to a passing private.

"Barkley! Fetch me a pigeon. And some toilet roll."

"Sir?"

"You heard me," said Babington, and Barkley saluted and hurried off.

Twenty minutes later, Max and Bentley looked on in satisfaction as the pigeon landed, followed by Babington's Avro.

It rolled to a halt, and Babington jumped down and walked across.

"Bloody marvellous. Don't know what we're going to wipe our arses with, but that's solved that. Well done, Edwards. HQ will be pleased with us," he said.

"Bit of a coo, you might say," said Bentley.

"Oh God," said Max.

October 1916

Max and Bentley landed wingtip to wingtip after an afternoon of chasing each other around the sky in mock dogfights, and taxied back to the hangars just as the sun slipped behind the horizon.

"Gosh, that was fun," said Bentley, "although of course I did kill you more times than you killed me."

"Aye, right," said Max as Babington came walking over.

"Bring your logbooks and training transfer-cards to me so I can sign them off, gentleman," he said. "Then pack your bags."

"Are we going on leave, sir?" said Bentley.

"Not exactly. A tender will collect you both at 0645 tomorrow to take you to the seven o'clock train, then direct to France via Newhaven and Dieppe."

"Oh bollocks," said Bentley, glancing at his watch as Babington walked away.

"What, because we're going to France?"

"No, because I've a date in ten minutes."

"Who, Angela from the Ship?"

"What? Lord, no. Angela was last month. Susan from the Red Lion. Would you mind awfully bringing my logbook and cards to Babington to sign? They're on the top shelf in my locker."

He hurried off, running his hand through his hair to straighten it, and Max shook his head and walked slowly towards their tent.

Chapter Nine

October 1916, two days later. Maranique airfield, France

Max and Bentley climbed out of the Crossley tender, stretched and looked at the scene before them.

"Welcome to paradise," said Bentley.

To their right, a row of jaunty Nieuport 11s and 17s with Lewis guns mounted on the top wings sat in front of a pair of large camouflaged tents. Compared to the Avro 504 sitting at the end of the row, they looked tiny but menacing.

To the other side were two semi-circular buildings made of corrugated iron and more dun-coloured tents of various sizes, and in the middle a wooden building like a smaller version of the one at Upavon.

In a wood at the edge of the field, magpies chattered, sounding disturbingly like machineguns.

A man in a Captain's uniform came limping towards them with the aid of a blackthorn stick, then stopped and stared at Max.

"Good God," he said. "Aren't you the infantryman who pulled me out of a burning kite in No Man's Land?"

"Good heavens. Yes, that was me."

"Well, in that case, I never got to shake your hand for saving my life," said the man, pumping it vigorously. "What's your name?"

"Max Edwards, sir. And this is Bentley Priory."

"Interesting name, Priory."

"He was named after a bluebell wood," said Max.

"Of course. I'm James Cox. Captain. The adjutant and recording officer. Let me take you to Major Cunningham, the CO."

He led them to the wooden building, and into a room at which a man who couldn't have been more than 30 sat at a desk. He looked unutterably weary.

"Edwards and Priory, sir," said Cox.

"Ah, yes. Thank you, Uncle," said the CO, then looked at Max and Bentley in turn.

"How many hours have you got?"

"Fifteen, sir," said Max.

"Nineteen, sir," said Bentley.

"And how many hours on scouts?"

"You mean single-seaters, sir?" said Bentley, and the CO nodded.

"Bugger all, sir," said Max. "Both of us."

"Sweet Christ. I thought CFS was supposed to be sending us pilots, not lambs to the slaughter," said Cunningham.

He buried his head in his hands, then ran his fingers through his hair.

"Never mind. You'd better make it bugger all squared before some clever Hun has you for breakfast, and then comes back for elevenses. Uncle will show you your quarters. Smyth!"

After a few moments, a door opened, and a face poked around it. The sort of face that was born with a sneer, and even its mother couldn't like. Behind it, Max caught a brief glimpse of a long table, a bar and walls hung with bits of German aeroplane. There was a gust of laughter, and a crash of breaking glass.

"Yes?" said the face.

The CO ignored the lack of a sir on the end.

"This is Edwards and Priory. Your latest heroes. Try not to lose them for at least a week, there's a good chap. Edwards and Priory, Smyth will be your flight commander. When Uncle shows you your quarters, Sergeant Rogerson will show you your kites. Take them up tomorrow and get used to them, then when Smyth thinks you're ready to be killed, he'll take you over the Lines."

"Do they know they're getting the sorriest excuses for aircraft available?" said Smyth.

"They do now," said Cunningham, then looked at Max and Bentley. "Gentlemen, do excuse our cynicism, but the average time from a pilot coming out to join our merry band and ending up in a pile of twisted metal is…what is it now, Uncle?"

"Eleven days, sir."

"Eleven sweet and happy days. So you see, there is little point in giving you decent aeroplanes."

"Like spending a lot of money on a coffin, really," said Smyth.

"Quite," said the CO. "Now, if you'll excuse me, I have to finish writing this letter to the proud parents of the poor fools you're replacing. If I can find some way of turning the fact that they crashed into each other on takeoff into bravely making the ultimate sacrifice with scant regard for their own safety in the valorous defence of King and Country."

"At least the bit about having scant regard for their own safety will be true," said Smyth.

"Indeed," said Cunningham, picking up his pen. "Dismissed. All of you."

"Charming," said Bentley as they walked away with Captain Cox.

"Indeed. A hearty welcome," said Max. "You're not really the CO's uncle, are you, sir?"

Cox laughed.

"No, it's just a term of infinite respect for my avuncular charm. Or possibly abuse," he said. "Right, let's dump your bags in that tent over there, and I'll take you on a tour of the highlights of the village. It won't take long, since there is only one."

They entered the tent to find two lockers, a small card table and a Private smoothing the blankets. He jumped to attention and saluted.

"Johnston, this is Second Lieutenants Edwards and Priory," said Uncle. "Chaps, just dump your kit on the beds. Johnston will see to it. We have more urgent business."

Ten minutes later, they had crossed the hump-backed river bridge on the edge of the airfield, walked down the single street of the little village at the edge of the airfield and were standing outside an estaminet with a faded sign above the door saying Jacinthe des bois, flanked by bluebells.

"Naturally, everyone calls it Jack's," said Uncle.

They walked inside, stooping through the door, and found themselves in a darkly atmospheric room, with the pale light through four windows along one wall falling on well-scrubbed wooden tables and simple chairs, and along the other wall a bar behind which stood a portly figure in a white apron polishing glasses.

"Oncle!" he said.

"Pierre, these are our latest young gentlemen, Messieurs Max and Bentley, and they would like a bottle of 1911 Château Margaux if your lovely whores upstairs haven't drunk it all."

"Oncle, you are very unkind. They are simply young ladies with a refreshing enthusiasm for the pleasures of the flesh. And a need to make a living, as we all do. However, you are in luck."

"Ah, possibly the finest sound in the known universe," said Cox as Pierre uncorked the bottle.

"I say, that's a bit lovely," said Max.

"Too right," said Bentley. "Drink up, for tomorrow we die."

"Or possibly the day after," said Uncle. "Let's remain optimistic while we can. Cheers."

"Cheers," said Max. "Why did you join up, by the way?"

"It seemed like a good idea at the time. And better than middle-aged spinsters presenting you with enough white feathers to make your own swan while you're walking down Oxford Street minding your own business," said Uncle. "What about you?"

"Trenchard told me to."

"Of course. Bentley?"

"They asked me at the interview if I rode, and I misunderstood the question. Is there really a brothel upstairs?" said Bentley.

"Of course. This is France, dear boy. A civilised country. However, if you're lucky enough to meet a young lady you don't have to pay, like some of the fragrant nurses from the hospital down the road, then there are a couple of bedrooms which Pierre rents out by the hour."

He paused, then took another large sip from his glass.

"That really is quite lovely. Or the half hour, if you're pushed."

The next morning, Smyth stuck his head around the door as they were at breakfast.

"Come with me," he said, and led them to a large tent in front of which stood two Nieuport 11s.

A Sergeant with his head buried in the cockpit of one looked up, saw them, jumped down and saluted.

"Where's Sergeant Rogerson, Simms?" said Smyth.

"Fred!" said Simms, and a middle-aged man with a face scarred by acne emerged from the tent, and saluted.

"Rogerson, this is Priory and Edwards. They're taking these two wrecks up to get used to them. Have them prepared."

As Rogerson was checking the machines, Smyth held out a packet of Kenilworth's. Bentley, who rarely smoked, took one to be polite.

"No thank you, sir. I don't," said Max.

"Everyone does. Good for the nerves."

"No thank you."

"Suit yourself. By the way, you didn't say what your father did."

"He's a butler, sir."

"Oh dear. How unfortunate for you. What about you, Priory?"

"Barrister, sir. Alexander Priory QC. You may have heard of him in the Maharajah of Jaipur case."

"No, don't believe I have."

Smyth tapped his cigarette on the back of his hand, and lit it, then Bentley's, and flicked the match away.

"What does yours do?" said Max.

"He's a lord. He doesn't have to do anything. Doing things is for other people," said Smyth as Rogerson came over.

"Both as ready as they're going to be, sir," he said.

* * *

Half an hour later, Max jumped down from the Nieuport as Rogerson came walking over.

"Well, sir, what do you think?"

"No harm to you, Fred, but this needs a bit of work," said Max, and Rogerson's mouth fell open.

"Sorry. I didn't mean to criticise your work," said Max. "Or the aeroplane."

"It's…it's not that, sir. It's just that the gentlemen don't use first names with the other ranks. Or even among themselves, from what I hear. They're very particular about it, sir."

"Lucky I'm not a gentleman, then," said Max. "Now here's what I want you to do. Rustle me up your best rigger and fitter, and we'll get to work on the flying wires. Then I want that right aileron adjusted. And the rudder, so I don't get cramp from stamping on the bar for hours on end."

"They all do that, sir. It's the effect of the rotary engine."

"Well, let's try and stop mine doing it, shall we?" said Max, then realised he sounded like Smyth, and stopped.

"Yes, sir."

"Then when we've done all that, we'll get to work on the engine. It sounds like a fight in a cutlery drawer."

"Yes, sir!" said Rogerson, then grinned and turned. "Blythe! Evans! Get your arses over here this minute, if not earlier!"

Blythe and Evans dropped their cigarettes, and came running, and Max climbed out to find Bentley walking over from his own Nieuport.

"How's yours?" said Max.

"Bit of a pig, to be honest. Engine sounds like a skeleton abusing itself in a tin bath."

Max laughed.

"Well, the CO did say we'd get the worst ones. Let's get mine sorted out, then we'll start on yours."

They finished both at 11 that night, and although it was too late for a test flight, ran up both engines.

"Well, bugger me with a rusty stick grenade. Sweet as a nut, sir," said Rogerson. "I take my hat off to you."

"Better than that. Let me buy you and the other chaps a pint to make up for missing dinner."

"That's very kind of you, sir, but we're not allowed in the officers' mess with the gentlemen."

"Then I'll buy you a pint in yours."

They emerged an hour later to find Smyth weaving his way back from dinner, obviously tight. He stopped, his face just as sardonic but even more aghast than usual.

"What the hell are you doing, Edwards?"

"Just buying Fred and the other chaps a pint to say thank you, sir."

"Fred? Who in the name of Christ is Fred?"

"Sergeant Rogerson, sir. And Blythe and Evans."

Smyth seized him by the arm and led him several yards away.

"Now listen to me, Edwards. You may only be the son of a butler, but you can at least try to pretend to be a gentleman. You are not to address NCOs by their first name. Or any of us, for that matter. And you are certainly not to drink with the riff-raff. Even if you are one of them. Is that understood?"

"Quite. Sir."

Smyth weaved off, and Max walked back to where Fred and Bentley were standing outside the NCO's mess.

"I do beg your pardon, sir. I've got you into trouble," said Fred.

"Not a bit of it, Fred. The man's a pillock of the highest order," said Max.

"Steady on. That's an insult to ordinary decent pillocks everywhere," said Bentley. "But he is a stuck-up prat. I bet he wears cufflinks on his pyjamas."

The next morning, Max and Bentley took the Nieuports up for another test flight.

"How is it, sir?" said Rogerson as Max climbed out.

"Much better. Good work. And say thank you to Blythe and Evans. By the way, who owns that nice Royal Enfield parked behind the mess?"

"Er, that was the young gentleman you replaced, sir."

"Ah. It's the 425cc V-Twin, isn't it? The Major had one back home."

"Tis indeed, sir. Last year's model. Bloody good idea putting the oil in a glass cylinder. Much better than total loss, and means you can check the level. "

"What's happening to it?"

"Well, he won't be needing it any more, sir. We won't be posting it home neither, so I imagine it's yours if you want it. It was running a bit rough, he said."

"Good stuff. I'll soon change that," said Max, as Bentley came walking over from his own test flight.

"Max, you are a genius and a half. Or possibly three quarters. That's a silk purse compared to the sow's ear it was yesterday," he said as Smyth came walking over with Robinson, one of the other flight leaders.

"I've been told to take you two up for some formation flying," he said. "Good stuff, formation flying. Crucial skill."

They went up, and stooged about pointlessly for an hour.

"Not too bad," said Smyth when they landed, "but you must stay closer."

"Surely if we're concentrating so hard on staying in formation, we're not looking out for enemy aircraft?" said Max.

"Don't be insolent, Edwards. Or any more than you have to. Right, I'll take you over the Lines tomorrow. In the meantime, I'll get Uncle to send a pigeon over telling the Huns they may as well surrender."

"What a pillock," muttered Bentley as he walked away. Smyth wheeled around.

"What did you say, Priory?"

"He said he thinks it's going to rain later, sir," said Max.

"I can always tell. Old family skill from when we were simple farming folk. In Somerset," said Bentley, and sniffed the air.

Smyth looked at both of them suspiciously, then turned and walked away.

"Oh arr," said Bentley.

Max had barely nodded off when he felt Johnston's hand shaking his shoulder.

"Six o'clock, sir. Rise and shine. Cup of tea for you."

Max groaned, and looked across at Bentley.

"What a bugger. I was having this lovely dream where a nurse I knew back home was just about to get her kit off and give me a bed bath," said Bentley.

"Could be worse, sir. Come the summer, you'll be up at three," said Johnston. "If you last that long."

"Is it just me," said Bentley, "or is everyone around here a gloomy bastard?"

An hour later, Max looked down from 10,000 ft through patchy cloud at dawn creeping over the wasteland where he had spent months wallowing in mud, blood, barbed wire and water, and marvelled that anyone could exist there, never mind fighting over it.

"What a complete and utter waste," he muttered over the roar of the engine, then looked across to see Smyth gesticulating furiously from his immaculate Nieuport 17 for him to stay in formation.

"Pillock!" he grinned cheerfully, waving back, then slid a couple of feet closer, just as a chrysanthemum of black smoke blossomed a hundred yards to their left, then another half a mile away, followed by a cough like a dragon clearing its throat.

Archie. Uncle had mentioned it the night before in the mess.

"Black is the Hun's. Not much to worry about. Rarely hits anything. White is ours, which is handy, because wherever you see white Archie, there be Huns," he'd said.

There was a rattle of machinegun fire, and he looked around in alarm and almost swerved into Smyth's machine, but it was only Smyth testing his Lewis gun.

He motioned for Max to do the same, and Max reached up, slid back the steel bar that acted as safety catch and dust cover, and squeezed the trigger on the Bowden cable.

There was a satisfying chatter, and he settled back down in the cockpit again and concentrated on keeping formation before he got another bollocking from Smyth.

They stooged on, and the Archie died away. Max kept an eye on his position, in between trying to scan the sky for other aircraft.

Then he saw a glint ahead and far below them, looked across at Smyth, waggled his wings and pointed.

Smyth peered, and shook his head.

Too far away, I imagine, thought Max, then looked again. It was a German two-seater sliding in and out of cloud, and he could just about see the observer looking up at him, then tapping the pilot on his shoulder.

The pilot looked back as well, then the aircraft dipped and began to dive away from them.

No harm in having a pop, thought Max, and stuck his nose down. He tilted his head left and right, then fired a three-second burst.

The German aircraft continued to dive as before, and he thought he had missed. Then it began to bank more steeply in a diving turn which turned into a steepening spiral as it fell faster and faster to the wasted earth below.

It hit the ground at full speed, and a tiny mushroom of orange and black blossomed and died.

Well, I never, thought Max, and slid back into position, then looked across at Smyth. Only to see a face cold with fury staring back at him.

He had hardly jumped to the ground after landing when Smyth was up to him, his gauntleted hand swinging high.

Max reached up and grabbed Smyth's wrist without thinking, and looked back into eyes glittering with vitriol.

"What the deuce is going on here?" came the CO's voice, and Smyth dropped his hand and stepped back.

"Edwards left formation. Without permission," he said.

"And shot down a Hun two-seater from about half a mile away," said Bentley, who had just walked up from his own aircraft.

"How far?"

"Beginner's luck, sir," said Max.

"All the same, I think you're to be congratulated rather than cursed," said the CO. "Smyth, I'll see you in my office in five minutes, if that doesn't inconvenience you."

"Sir," said Smyth, then glanced bitterly at Max and strode off, pulling off his gloves as he walked away.

"He means well, but…" said the CO, then looked at Max, whose teeth were chattering. "Is that fear, or a reaction to the bracing temperatures up there?"

"It was, um, refreshing, sir," said Max.

"Your nose has gone a fascinating shade of blue," said Bentley. "Time for a nice cup of tea, I think."

"Is there a seamstress in the village, Uncle?" said Max as he huddled over a mug in the mess.

"Yes, Madame Voillet. Why?"

"I'm going to buy a couple of sheep, turn them inside out and get her to make me a nice warm suit."

"Good idea. Make one for me as well, then we can have the sheep for supper," said Bentley, then glanced at his watch.

"Heavens, look at the time. Better get cracking. I've an urgent appointment tonight in Jack's with a sweet little nurse from the hospital down the road. Pamela, from Croydon. Uncle was right."

Max watched him go, wondering how on earth he'd managed that, then went to his tent, lay down on the camp bed and was fast asleep in five minutes.

Chapter Ten

The next day

"Ah, that's more like it," said Max, looking down at the German two-seater trundling along a thousand feet below.

He looked across at Smyth, and pointed. Smyth nodded, and looked up and behind them, but they were bouncing along under a layer of cloud, and there was nothing to be seen.

He tipped the nose of the Nieuport down, and Max and Bentley followed suit in tight formation.

The German observer spotted them, and a stream of bullets flickered up to meet them, then danced past, but Smyth never flinched.

He may be a pillock, but he's a brave pillock, thought Max, just as a row of bullet holes marched along the wing to where he was sitting.

He kicked the rudder hard and pulled the stick back.

He was only just in time. The instrument panel shattered in a bright splintering of brass and wood, and as his plane reared and slowed, an all-black Albatros slid below.

For a moment he felt as if he was looking over the edge of a rowing boat at a cruising shark, then his left wing dropped sharply and the earth and sky began to spin crazily.

"What the —" he said as his world alternated giddily between brown and blue, then began to turn grey and red as a mist descended across his eyes.

Half out of instinct and half of panic, he kicked the rudder bar hard in the opposite direction to the way the world was rotating.

That, at least, stopped the spinning, and his vision cleared to the extent where he could see that the aircraft was wallowing on the edge of stalling and spinning in the opposite direction.

He centralised the rudder, then pushed the stick forward. With the wind over the wings, the machine started flying again.

"Good grief," said Max. "That was bloody close. I wonder if I've accidentally worked out how to get out of a spin."

He flew back to the field, banked left and right, and looked all around him. The sky was empty, and he was still at 10,000 ft, so he had plenty of altitude to play with.

Taking a deep breath, he pulled the stick back, and kicked the rudder bar, and his machine paused for effect, then started spinning again. He let the earth spin twice, then reversed what he had done before. Then did it again the other way, just to prove it had been luck.

"Bloody hell. This is going to make me old before my time," he said, and landed.

"What exactly were you doing up there this afternoon, Edwards?" said the CO in the mess that evening.

"Spinning practice, sir. We were never really taught it at CFS, and I only discovered how to get out by accident earlier yesterday."

"Shame. We could all have had a good laugh when you buried yourself and saved us the trouble in a week or two," said Smyth, who was on his fourth or fifth gin at the bar.

"Shut up, Smyth," said the CO. "You were bloody lucky. How many times have I told you that two-seaters stooging about without a care in the world are just a decoy for scouts waiting above for a mug to come along?"

"Several, sir," said Smyth, then signalled the steward and pointed to his empty glass.

"He's a bit cut up tonight," said Uncle. "Robinson went west this afternoon. Flamer about ten miles into Hunland. He and Smyth had been best pals since Eton."

"Oh dear," said Max, then got up and walked over to Smyth. He was just about to put his hand on the other man's shoulder, then thought better of it.

Smyth turned and glared at him.

"Yes?"

"I'm sorry to hear about Robinson, sir. I didn't even get to know him very well. What was his first name?"

Smyth stared at him.

"How the hell would I know?" he said.

The following evening, with low cloud and rain stopping play and everyone getting merry in the mess, except for Bentley, who had set off to Jack's hoping to move his relationship with Pamela upstairs, Max was looking at the map of the area on the wall when he suddenly remembered what Bentley had said about the hospital down the road.

"Uncle, is that hospital you were talking about Base Hospital 84?"

"What?" said Uncle. "Yes, through the village and about ten miles down the road. Why?"

But Max was already out the door and climbing on the Royal Enfield.

He parked it outside, walked in and looked around to find his bearings, then made his way to Matron's office and tapped on the door.

She looked up as he walked in, took a moment to recognise him, then smiled.

"Monsieur Edwards! Êtes-vous bien?"

"Beaucoup mieux, grâce à vous, Matron. Is Yvette still here?"

"Yes, in the same ward. You remember where it is?"

"How could I forget? It is where I met you, after all."

She gave him a mock frown, and he grinned and walked down the corridor, his footsteps clicking on the polished marble.

Yvette was facing away from him, dressing a patient's leg, and he closed the door quietly behind him and waited until she turned and saw him. Her hand went to her mouth.

"Oh!"

He walked to her.

"Pleased, or surprised?" he said.

"Both." She glanced down at his wings. "Ah, you have taken flight. How is it?"

"A lot better than the trenches."

"I can imagine. What are you doing here?"

"My squadron is stationed at Maranique, and I just wanted to thank you for saving me from certain death."

"Ha!" she tilted her head and smiled. "It was only a scratch."

"Of course. Men make such a fuss. Are you free this evening?"

She tilted her head.

"Why?"

"I wanted to take you out to dinner. I hear the Savoy in Amiens is lovely."

"Oh dear."

"What?" he said, his heart sinking. Of course. She's so pretty she must already have a boyfriend.

"I am working every evening. Is Saturday possible?"

"Saturday is very possible," he said, and kissed her hand. "Would you like to travel by motorcycle, or in a boring old Crossley tender if I can liberate one?"

"Oh, motorcycle. Much more exciting! I am not too far from Maranique. Here, I will write you directions."

Chapter Eleven

The following Saturday, Amiens

"What a wonderful meal," she said as they walked by the canal after a nightcap in Charlie's Bar.

"Stunning. That beef flambéed in whiskey. And your duck. And the truffles. And you," said Max.

"You are very sweet," she laughed. "I enjoyed every minute of it."

"Me too," he said, looking at her in the moonlight. She was wearing a white cotton dress with little Michaelmas daisies all over it and a lace collar. She looked heartmendingly beautiful.

"You look very fine in your uniform," she said.

"And you look very fine out of yours," he said.

She laughed, and they leaned on the railings and looked at the moon dancing in the Somme. How strange, he thought, that this peaceful scene should share the same name as the maelstrom of mud and blood.

"Good grief," he said, looking at his watch. "I'd better be getting you home. Won't you be cold in that dress?"

"No, I am fine, thank you."

"Take my jacket anyway. It'll keep you cosy."

She put it on, and wrapped her arms around him as they set off on the Enfield, with her sitting on the makeshift pillion seat of his service coat strapped to the luggage rack. It felt very fine as they puttered home along the poplar-lined road out of Amiens, with the full moon above.

On one horizon, the thunder and lightning of nature split the sky, and on the other the thunder and lightning of the man-made barrage tried to match it, but in the middle, all was still apart from the syncopated heartbeat of the Enfield's engine, and above that the heartbeats of Max and Yvette as she held him close.

Half an hour later, they pulled to a halt outside the little gate lodge of the manor house where her parents lived.

She got off the back of the bike, and he put the stand down and stood before her in the breathing dark, uncertain whether he should kiss her or not.

She solved the issue by standing on her tiptoes and kissing him. Her mouth opened, their tongues intertwined, and for a moment Max was giddy with the taste of her, the lavender scent of her eau de cologne and the softness of her dress where his hand pressed it gently into the small of her back.

She pulled back and looked up at him in the moonlight for several seconds.

"Would you like to stay?" she said at last.

"That would be very nice," said Max.

Inside, she went to the bathroom, and he undressed and climbed into her big brass bed. Uncertain whether to take off his underpants, he dithered for a moment, then draped them over the back of a chair with his other clothes.

Moments passed. The fat moon looked in through the window. He held his breath as the bathroom door opened and Yvette walked across the room. She was wearing a white nightdress, then turned and lifted it over her head. His heart stopped at her slim, pale beauty.

"Close your eyes," she said, and he did, then felt the covers lift and the bed sink as she climbed in beside him.

They kissed, again, and he marvelled at the feeling of her against him, aware of a swelling excitement down below.

"Gosh. This is lovely," he said. "I hadn't a clue what it was going to be like."

She lifted her head, and looked at him.

"You mean this is your first time?"

He nodded.

"Oh Max. That is so sweet. Well then, let us be slow and gentle. I want you to kiss me everywhere, and I will tell you what to do if you need."

Much as he had marvelled before, he marvelled again now, at the softness of her breasts on his lips, the hardness of her nipples, the soft down on her belly, the crisp dark hair below, and then the delicious confusion of flesh. She opened like a flower in rain to let his tongue slide in, and told him what to do.

How exquisite this is, he thought. The intimacy and gentle precision of it.

After a while her breath began to quicken, and then she stiffened, arched and shuddered with a sudden, surprising gasp.

"Mon dieu," she whispered at last. "Max, you are a wonder."

"Thank you," said Max. "That was quite the loveliest thing that's ever happened to me."

"Oh no it is not," she laughed. "Now I will return the favour."

She rolled him onto his back, and bent over him.

"Gosh," said Max afterwards. "It's amazing how much fun you can have with just two naked bodies."

They fell asleep in each other's arms, and the last thing Max remembered thinking before he nodded off was that apart from flying, this was probably the only thing he had not learned from reading a book in the library at Termon.

"You know," she said, snuggled under his chin after they woke the next morning, "I have promised to myself that I will wait to do everything with a man only when I marry him, so would it be all right if we just do…other things?"

"You mean other things like last night?"

He felt her head nod under his chin.

"Well, as far as I remember, they seemed entirely lovely to me. Although…"

"Although what?"

"You know, something terrible has happened. I seem to have lost my memory, and have forgotten how lovely."

"Heavens, that is terrible. I must remind you," she said, then squeezed his arm and disappeared under the covers.

Chapter Twelve

November 1916

They popped out of the cloud at 15,000 ft over Polygon Wood, and Max gasped.

Ahead of them, seven of the new S.E.5s were slugging it out with ten or so Halberstadts. Two thousand feet below that, a dozen Pfalzes were fighting off about thirty British scouts of varying types, below that, about thirty Albatri were whirling around a dozen or so DH.2s, and below that again, a flight of German two-seaters was cruising along in the direction of Ypres without a care in the world.

"Good grief. It looks like the entire German Air Force, and most of ours," he muttered, and looked across at Smyth for a clue as what to do.

In answer, Smyth stuck the nose down and headed straight for the DH.2s, who were most in need of help.

They fell out of the sky, their engines racing and the wind howling through the rigging wires like a banshee. Max glanced at his airspeed indicator to see the needle jammed against the stop. He didn't dare glance at the wings, but so far they were still on.

And then, suddenly, they were in the thick of it. A yellow Albatros flashed in front of him, and he slammed the rudder bar, skidded and gave it a burst which missed by a mile.

A bonfire which only a few seconds ago had presumably been an aeroplane with a living and breathing human being in it hurtled past his nose, and his nostrils filled with a sick whiff of charred hope as he shot through its trail.

A white Albatros slid past on his right as if in a dream, tight on the tail of a DH.2. The pilot of the British aircraft suddenly slumped in his seat, and the DH.2 twitched and soared. The Albatros, too close to avoid it, chewed its way into the tail of the DH.2 and they fell away, locked together in death.

A DH.2 shot over his head with a green and black Albatros in hot pursuit, its guns blazing, and he ducked then looked up and winced as a purple German machine with a yellow tail shot in front of him.

It vanished as quickly as it had appeared, and his ears were filled with the rattle of machinegun fire from somewhere. He looked down, and realised his thumb was jammed hard on the trigger.

He lifted it, the noise stopped, and he saw a mauve Albatros in front of him on the tail of another DH.2. It was so close that he couldn't miss, and he squeezed the trigger again. The Lewis chattered for a few seconds, then stopped. Jammed. He hammered on the drum with his gloved hand, but it was too late.

He watched helplessly, his heart sinking, at the white face of the DH.2 pilot looking over his shoulder at his nemesis.

A moment later, the entire rear section of the DH.2 crumpled, and the doomed aircraft fluttered down like an autumn leaf.

Max watched it fall, then looked up for the mauve Albatros. It was nowhere to be seen, and neither was anything else.

Where a minute before the entire sky had been filled with hurtling, blazing, roaring aircraft and flying metal, it was now utterly empty.

Max shook his head, steadied the aircraft until the compass stopped spinning, then turned for home.

At the airfield, he breathed a sigh of relief to see Bentley and Smyth's aircraft already there, then landed without incident and jumped down as Rogerson came walking over.

"Still alive, sir?" he grinned.

"Just about, Fred. Flipping gun jammed, so from now on we're going to check every single bullet that goes into that drum."

"As you wish, sir."

"In fact, I've had a better idea. Reinforce the centre section of the top wing and stick two Lewis guns on it, with a Bowden cable leading to a single trigger. Give me twice the firepower," said Max, looking up to see Bentley trotting over with a broad smile on his face.

"What are you looking so happy about?"

"Got behind an Albatros and gave him what for, that's what. What a flipping ding-dong that was. One minute it was Dante's Inferno, the next it was Swan Lake in an empty sky."

"Wish I'd got something. My gun jammed just when I had one bang to rights."

"But you did."

"What?"

"That purple one with the yellow tail. It shot in front of you, then went straight down. Fell into Polygon Wood at a rate of knots."

"Bloody hell. I was too busy avoiding it to notice."

"A kill each. Next stop Jack's," said Bentley.

The next afternoon, they were about ten miles over the Lines when Bentley waggled his wings and pointed.

"Good spot, chum," said Max, picking up what looked like half a dozen German aircraft several miles ahead and about a thousand feet below.

Smyth lowered his nose, and the three dipped as one, the wind whistling through the wires as they fell on the unsuspecting aircraft, which as they got closer looked like Pfalzes.

Max picked out the one on the far left, a pink and green affair, and when he heard the chatter of Smyth's guns to his right, squeezed the trigger which fired both Lewis guns.

The enemy pilot seemed to sit bolt upright in his seat, then the Pfalz soared to the left and began a long fall to earth.

Max pulled the Nieuport hard up and around in a chandelle, and came racing back at another Pfalz. The two aircraft thundered towards each other, guns blazing, and just as a crash seemed inevitable, Max froze, closed his eyes and waited to die.

Then opened them to find he was still alive.

"If only Fido was here to see this," he said, for no reason at all, then laughed hysterically with relief and turned to chase the Pfalz again, but the sky was empty. It had happened again.

Suddenly Smyth popped up out of nowhere, followed by Bentley, and Smyth pointed for home.

They were cruising along at 12,000 ft when Max spotted the Albatros two-seater stooging back and forward over the British lines, obviously taking photographs.

He waggled his wings and pointed, and Smyth pointed at his gun and made a zero with his thumb and forefinger. Out of ammunition.

Max pointed at himself, then at the Albatros, Smyth nodded, and Max put the Nieuport on its side and curved down and below the Albatros,

He tilted the Lewis guns skyward on the curved rack, locked them in place, pressed the trigger and eased the stick back, then watched with a grim satisfaction bordering on horror as after a two-second burst, the entire centre section of the enemy two-seater disintegrated where his bullets had hit it.

"That's more like it," he said, then climbed back to join the other two, only to see Smyth gesticulating furiously for him to get back into formation.

"Silly bastard," said Max as a puff of black smoke mushroomed in front of them. Archie. His Nieuport rose and fell as it passed through the gust of hot air left by the blast, and his nostrils were filled with a brief, acrid whiff of cordite as other dark clouds blossomed around them, then vanished behind.

Nothing much to worry about, he thought. As Uncle said, Archie rarely did any damage. Complete waste of time, really.

Suddenly there was a deafening crack, and he looked across to see the entire centre section of Smyth's Nieuport disappear in a cloud of black.

For a moment the aircraft maintained its shape, either to maintain its essential being as an aeroplane or to follow to the end Smyth's obsession with tight formation, and then the wings and tail section broke off and fluttered away, leaving the nose to begin a long plunge to earth with the propeller still rotating idly. Of Smyth in the middle, there was no sign.

"Archie 1, Pillocks of the World 0," said Bentley in Jack's that night, raising a glass of cognac just as a pretty blonde walked through the door, saw him and waved.

"Samantha!" said Bentley, holding up the bottle and waving it back, then making a glass shape with his free hand. Samantha went to the bar to get one.

"Don't tell me, another nurse," said Max.

"Endless supply of them, chum. That's what hospitals are for, although to Sam's credit, she's also an expert in the workings of the internal combustion engine," said Bentley.

"Really?"

"Absolutely. She was demonstrating it to me upstairs last night. Suck, squeeze, bang, blow," grinned Bentley.

Max buried his head in his hands and mock-wept as Samantha kissed Bentley and sat down, then took a compact mirror out of her handbag and refreshed her lipstick.

"You know," said Max, "that's given me an idea."

"Don't be silly. That colour wouldn't suit you," said Bentley, pouring Samantha a very large cognac.

"Gosh. Are you trying to get me squiffy and have your evil way with me?" she said.

"Thought never crossed my mind, dear. But now that you mention it," said Bentley.

"No, I mean the mirror," said Max.

The next day, he found Rogerson servicing his engine.

"Fred!"

"Sir?"

"I've had an idea, and since it doesn't happen too often, I wanted you to be the first to know."

"I'm honoured, sir."

"So you should be. See if you can dig up a small mirror from somewhere, and bolt it to that strut just in front of the cockpit."

"What for, sir?"

"So I can see what a dangerous future I have behind me," said Max, then looked at his watch. Yvette would be finishing her shift about now. Perfect.

He had a cup of tea in the mess, then rode over on the Enfield, arriving just as she climbed out of a handsome cream Renault in front of the manor house.

He got off the motorcycle and walked over as her parents got out. Her father, a surgeon at the hospital in Amiens, was a handsome man with hair greying at the edges, and her mother was exactly like an older version of Yvette.

"Mama and Papa, this is Max, who I told you about," said Yvette, and Max stepped forward and held out his hand.

"Honoured to meet you, sir," he said in his by now passable French. M. Leroy-Beaulieu's handshake was as cool and firm as his daughter's.

"The pleasure is mine. Yvette has been telling us about you. This is Sylvie, her mother. Who also happens to be my wife."

Max laughed, took Mme. Leroy-Beaulieu's hand, and kissed it.

"Delighted. I see now where Yvette gets her beauty from," he said.

"Max! Stop trying to seduce my mother," said Yvette, cuffing him on the elbow. "But at least your French is improving."

"I was trying to praise her daughter," said Max, and Yvette's father laughed.

"Nice recovery," he said. "Will you join us for dinner? Boeuf en croute, and a very nice claret."

My God, thought Max as they walked towards the house and Yvette and her mother took one of his hands each. I'm turning into Bentley.

"CO wants to see you. Both of you," said Uncle, sticking his head around the door of their hut the next day.

"Oh bollocks. What have we done now?" said Bentley.

They found Cunningham at his desk, scribbling as usual.

"Ah, you two," he said, looking up. "With Smyth gone, I'd better move one of you up to full Lieutenant, but after what Smyth said about how appalling you both were at staying in formation, I can't decide who'll do the least damage."

"Didn't do Smyth much good, Sir," said Max.

"Don't be insolent, Edwards."

Max and Bentley shuffled awkwardly as the CO shuffled some papers on his desk, then looked up.

"Oh God. I may as well make it both of you. I'll send the paperwork through tomorrow, and let the Germans know they may as well surrender now."

"I think this calls for a celebration," said Bentley as they walked away. "Fancy a snifter in Jack's?"

"Don't you have a date with one of your nurses?"

"I'm having a night off, so looks like it's your lucky night."

"Shame I'm a lesbian," said Max, "but let's get Uncle to come along as chaperone just in case."

"Lesbians are homosexuals, you know. I remember reading somewhere that the word comes from the Greek for the same, not the Latin for men," said Bentley.

"Yes, yes, I know that," said Max.

"So does that mean if I sleep with one, I like men?" said Bentley.

"I doubt it," said Max. "But I'll keep a revolver under my pillow just in case."

December 1916

"Anything in the paper?" said Bentley, coming back from the mess bar with a bottle of St Julien and two glasses.

"Another big push, back to where we started," said Max, then glanced at the date on top of the page. "Mind you, this is a week old, so anything could have happened since then. Hang on a second. What date is it?"

"Haven't a clue, old bean. I think it's still 1916."

Max did a quick calculation.

"Good God," he said. "I've just realised it's Christmas Eve."

"Bollocks and buggery. We'd better hang up our stockings, then get down to Jack's. No, wait, I've a better idea. Let's bring our stockings down to Jack's and see if we can find someone to fill them."

"Bloody lucky I spotted that. Yvette's parents have invited me over for Christmas lunch tomorrow," said Max as they shrugged on their British Warms and set out into the frozen night.

"You might get a big push yourself then, you lucky dog. I haven't had one for a week. I'll be turning back into a virgin if this keeps up," said Bentley.

"Shut up, Bentley. You're absolutely disgusting," said Max. "There are other things to life than sex, you know."

"You're right, chum. When I was young and foolish, I thought of nothing else, but now that I'm older and wiser, I do see that the other one per cent of life matters too."

Chapter Thirteen

January 1917

"Late Christmas present, sir," said Fred, wiping his hands with an oily rag which only made them more oily and looking at the row of Sopwith Pups which had just been delivered.

"Very nice," said Bentley. "What do you think?"

"Looks a bit more purposeful than the Nieuport," said Max. "How does the performance compare, Fred?"

"Same 80-horse Le Rhône rotary, sir. Service ceiling 17,500 feet instead of 15,000 or so, and gets there faster, so I'm told."

"Is that the new synchronization thing?" said Bentley, poking around the single Vickers mounted in front of the cockpit.

"Tis indeed, sir. Sopwith-Kauper. Stops you shooting the propeller off, which is generally a good thing."

"About time we had one. The Huns have had one for almost two flipping years," said Max. "Good stuff. We'll take it up and try it out tomorrow."

As they cruised over the ruins of Albert the next morning, Max looked down and saw the morning sun glint off the leaning virgin, the golden statue of Mary and the infant Jesus which had been hanging almost horizontally from the top of the Basilica of Notre-Dame de Brebières for the past two years after being hit by a shell.

The British said that whoever made the statue fall would lose the war, and the Germans thought the opposite.

Lucky Bentley can't get at the virgin, thought Max, or it wouldn't stand a chance.

And then he caught another glint, further to the east. He looked over at Bentley, and pointed, and Bentley peered into the rising sun, then nodded.

They lowered the noses of the Pups, and crept stealthily down, and as they got closer, the glint materialised into three Albatros scouts: the black one which had almost shot Max down, a white one with an ace of spades on the side, and a black one with a skull and crossbones on the side and a white tail.

Looks like the devil and his chums out for a morning constitutional, thought Max, as they slipped quietly into the blind spot behind and under the German aircraft.

They were now only 50 yards ahead, and still cruising on without a care in the world.

I'm fed up telling the chaps to keep a good lookout, thought Max as he cocked the Vickers, eased the stick back, watched the centre section of the rear Albatros drift into the Aldis sight, and squeezed the trigger.

The German reared, then veered violently to the left and began to dive away. Max chased it down, hearing behind him the rattle of Bentley's Vickers as he fired at one of the other Huns.

He closed in on the white tail of the Albatros, watching it bob about in front of him as the pilot jinked and weaved, then squeezed the trigger as it filled his vision.

The Vickers rattled for a couple of seconds, and the Albatros fell into a spin with smoke pouring from the engine, then there was a bang and the Pup started trying to shake itself to pieces.

"Bloody hell, bloody hell," said Max. His first thought was that he had been hit, but a glance in his mirror then over each shoulder revealed an empty sky.

He throttled back, and the vibrating eased a bit, so it was either engine or propeller trouble.

Nursing it at as low revs as possible, he turned for home, losing height all the way.

He was never going to make it home. He tried opening up the revs again, but it was impossible. He was going to have to put her down.

He looked ahead, but the ground was just a mess of smoke, tree stumps, ruined hedges and corpses.

Then to the left he spotted a patch of clear ground about the size of a couple of tennis courts, and tilted as gently as he could towards them.

Hold off, hold off, and he was down and rolling to a stop beside a trench. He switched off the engine, and with the prop stopped, he could see one of the blades badly splintered where his bullets had hit it.

He sat there, his ears buzzing with the sudden silence, and looked over to the trench to see whether he was to be saved or made a prisoner.

A pair of tin helmets popped up, followed by their owners, and he breathed a sigh of relief.

"You all right, sir?" said one of the soldiers.

"Absolutely. I just got fed up flying, and decided I'd join you lot for a bit," said Max.

"Wouldn't recommend it, sir, to be honest," said the other one.

"Engine trouble, sir?" said Rogerson as Max climbed down from the tender back at Maranique.

"Sopwith-Kauper trouble. That thing's bloody useless. When you bring the Pup back, take the Vickers off and put my twin Lewis guns on the top wing again."

He looked up to see Bentley's Pup curving in to land from afternoon patrol.

It taxied up, and Bentley climbed out and walked over.

"Been on holiday?"

"Of course. Shot my prop off. Where did you get to?"

"Oh, it was a laugh and a half. After you scarpered, I had a regular old ding-dong with the rest of the black tie brigade until a handful of S.E.5s turned up and chased them off," he said. "Hope they don't make you pay for your prop. Fancy a small brandy?"

"Good idea. Then we can use the rest of the bottle to make a pyre for that pile of synchronizer junk," said Max.

March 1917

"Jesus, this tea's awful. Johnston, do you pee in it or something?" said Bentley.

"Probably improve it, sir. It's the condensed milk, I'm afraid. Can't get fresh," said Johnston.

"What we need's a cow," said Max. "I'll have a word with Yvette's parents."

That evening, Bentley was sitting in the mess with his feet up reading the Daily Telegraph when there was a polite cough outside the door.

He opened it to find Max holding a rope. To the other end was attached a large black and white Friesian.

"Bentley, Gertrude. Gertrude, Bentley," said Max.

Gertrude was installed on a quiet corner of the field, a milking rota tacked to the noticeboard in the mess, and the tea improved.

A week later, Max was taxiing in to land when he glanced over at Gertrude and began to laugh. On her flank was a large red, white and blue roundel.

He switched off, jumped down and found Blythe putting the lid back on a tin of red paint.

"Michael, have you been having designs on Gertrude?"

"Thought you'd approve, sir," grinned Blythe.

Chapter Fourteen

April 1917

Max had shot down a couple of barrage balloons and in the absence of any other action was pottering home at 15,000 ft through patchy cloud.

Below, the barrage on both sides was going full pelt, guided by an R.E.8 on one side of the Lines and a DKW on the other, and the entire earth flickered and danced with the light of guns firing and shells bursting.

"Glad I'm up here," he said to himself, then glanced down again and saw an Albatros with olive green and mauve wings and a yellow fuselage diving after two Nieuports.

"You're game," he said and stuck the nose of the Pup down.

The common wisdom was that nine out of ten pilots never saw the man who killed them, and so it proved for the unfortunate occupant of the rear Nieuport.

It reared as the Albatros poured a stream of bullets into it, then began to spiral down to earth with smoke pouring from the engine.

The pilot of the other Nieuport looked over his shoulder, then and jinked left and right to shake off his attacker, but the Albatros closed in like a terrier after a rat.

"He's bloody good," said Max, and although he was still further away than he would have liked, he sent a speculative stream of bullets arcing towards the Albatros more to get the pilot off the Nieuport's tail than anything else.

The Albatros pilot glanced around, then pulled the stick back, cut the throttle to kill his speed and looked down as Max hurtled past below him.

"Clever," said Max, then watched in his mirror as the Albatros began to slide into place for the kill, and flicked the Pup into a spin.

At 10,000 ft he levelled out briefly, only to see the red spinner of the Albatros appear again in his mirror. Its twin Spandaus flashed, something plucked at his sleeve and his altimeter disappeared in a bright shower of shards.

"Christ, he is good," muttered Max grimly, and spun the Pup the other way until fields filled his vision.

He centred the controls, then gasped as a row of poplars lining a road filled his vision. He jerked the stick to one side, missed the first tree by inches, steadied the Pup, raced down the road at six feet and rounded a sweeping bend only to see a farmer's horse and cart piled high with something straight ahead of him.

He lifted the Pup up and over it, caught a brief whiff of manure, and in his mirror caught a glimpse of the horse galloping down the road with the farmer standing up hauling on the reins.

He looked to his right, and saw the Albatros racing along on the other side of the trees, the pilot looking at him as they flickered from light to shade and back again.

Then, half a mile ahead, he saw his escape: a crossroads, with a gap in the trees. At the last second, he blipped the engine briefly, then pulled the Pup up and hard to the right, holding his breath as branches lashed the undercarriage and Lewis guns on the top wing, then flicked hard down and left, saw the tail of the Albatros only yards ahead, and squeezed the trigger.

Nothing happened. He was out of ammunition.

He watched helplessly as the Albatros banked hard to the right, curved around and slid in behind him, then hunched down in his cockpit and closed his eyes, waiting for the coup de grace. Long seconds passed.

Max opened his eyes, and looked to the right to see the Albatros glide alongside, on its pale yellow fuselage a red heart edged in white and a green laurel wreath with a swastika inside.

The pilot pushed up his goggles, grinned across at Max, pointed to his guns and made a circle with his gloved fingers. Nothing. He was out of ammunition as well. He looked about sixteen years old.

Max breathed for the first time in what seemed like several minutes, shrugged and saluted, and the other man saluted back, then swung away.

Max watched him go, then scanned the empty sky and turned for home.

"What beautiful aircraft they have. Ours are so drab by comparison," he said.

"Been having fun, sir?" said Fred, stooping to pull several small branches out of the undercarriage.

"Absolutely. Nothing like it," said Max, then went to the CO and asked if he could brighten up his kite by painting the tail.

"No," said the Old Man, and that was the end of it.

"That was Voss," said Uncle, when Max described the Albatros in the mess that evening. "In which case you're lucky to be alive."

"Voss?" said Max.

"Werner," said Uncle. "Still only nineteen and with twenty five victories on his bedpost. The boy wonder."

"That's even more than you, Bentley. At least you don't usually kill your girlfriends."

"No. Although they'd probably kill me if they found out about each other," said Bentley.

"I'm sure they do anyway," said Max. "Women are smarter than you think."

"Secret of happiness," said Uncle. "Find a woman who is loving and tender. Find a woman who makes you laugh. Find a woman who can cook. And find a woman you can trust. And most of all, make sure these four women never meet."

"Yes, very good, Uncle," laughed Max.

"That's because you haven't heard it before," said the CO.

The next evening, he was walking idly around the airfield when he came upon Blythe, sitting by the river with an easel painting the sunset.

"That's very impressive, Michael. You're a man of hidden talents," he said, bending to inspect it.

"Thank you, sir. Some of them are even useful," said Blythe. "To be honest, I wanted to go to art college, but we couldn't afford it. Dad was having none of it anyway. Not a proper job, he said. So he made me serve an engineering apprenticeship."

"Mmm. I know how you feel, if it's any consolation. But don't give that up. That's a rare skill," said Max, and walked away, then stopped, took the little lilac bag out of his pocket, and slid Kumiko's carp out of it.

"Michael, do you think you could paint this on the side of my cockpit?" he said, handing it over and feeling a faint twinge of loss at having it out of his possession for even a moment.

"Gosh, what a beautiful piece. Of course. I'll take a crack at it," said Blythe.

"Although not too big, or the Old Man will have a fit," said Max, then retrieved the carp, slid it safely back into his pocket, and walked on.

"Perfect. Absolutely perfect," said Max the next day as he and Bentley admired Blythe's handiwork.

Bentley coughed, and Max looked around to see the CO standing behind them.

"Edwards, I thought I told you specifically not to decorate your aircraft," he said.

"It's…not a decoration, sir," said Max. "Good luck charm. Based on the old family motto. Carpe diem."

"Seize the fish," said Bentley helpfully.

"You two will be the death of me," said Cunningham.

"Nonsense, sir. We're on your side," said Max.

"There are times when I doubt it," said the CO, then bent to look at the carp. "Oh well, I suppose it can't do any harm."

"Was that true, sir? About the carp, I mean," said Blythe.

"Don't be silly, Blythe. It was a red herring," said Bentley.

"Sob," said Max.

The next day, Max was sitting on a bench in the sun checking ammunition belts when he looked up to see a Nieuport curve in to a beautiful landing.

The pilot got out, and strolled over. He had a big, rugged way about him, with dark brown hair and deep-set blue eyes in a handsome, worried face.

"Nice landing," said Max.

"Grand job, so. I'm looking for the lad who chased a yellow bird off my tail over Albert a couple of days back," said the newcomer in a thick accent.

"Ah. That was me. Sorry about your other fellow."

"He was supposed to be watching me arse, the useless shite. Scared the crap out of me. It was only his second time up. Crash landed and broke his legs. Lucky he didn't go down a flamerino."

He tilted his head and looked at Max.

"You from the North?"

"Aye, Tyrone."

"Cork, meself."

"Aye, I'd worked that out."

The other man laughed, and held out a square hand.

"Edward Mannock. Or Mick, if you like."

"Max Edwards."

Mannock crushed Max's hand, then looked up at the sky.

"How you finding it?"

"Better than the trenches."

"Oh? Who were you with?"

"36th Ulster."

"Jaysus. At the Somme?"

Max nodded.

"I was one of the lucky ones. Took a bullet on the first day."

"Frigging nightmare, I heard. How many did you lose?"

"Good question. I heard two thousand dead. Three thousand injured."

"What a cock-up that was. I was Engineers. Not so bad. Then this lot. Mind you, nearly killed myself spinning a DH.2 on my first solo before I figured my way out of it. Thank Christ I remembered Mac's advice."

"McCudden? What was it?"

"Centre the controls and say a small prayer."

Max laughed.

"You're lucky. My instructor died of a heart attack on my first lesson."

Mannock threw back his head.

"Ha! Sounds like we're both lucky bastards, then. The CO thought I was showing off until I showed him the state of me pants, so."

He paused.

"Anyway, the flying's great. It's the other stuff that scares the shite out of me. Especially burning. I'll shoot myself if that ever happens," he said as Bentley came up.

"Bentley, Edward Mannock. Mick, Bentley Priory," said Max.

"What sort of a name's that?" said Mannock.

"The sort of name you should buy a drink," said Bentley, and Mannock laughed and slapped him on the back.

"You're on, so," he said.

Chapter Fifteen

July 1917

It was a glorious Sunday afternoon, and he and Yvette lay in a buttercup meadow by the river, dazed and happy after a picnic of baguette, runny Brie, pâté and a perfect bottle of Pouilly-Fumé.

Max was half-dozing, and Yvette was leaning on an elbow, looking down at the river.

"What do you think you will do after the war, darling?" she said.

"What? Oh. I don't even like to think about it too much, love. Or even tomorrow. Bad luck to tempt fate."

He was silent for a moment. A bee wavered past.

"I suppose stay in the RFC if it needs me, although I suspect there'll be a quart of pilots trying to squeeze into a pint of jobs if peace ever happens. Or go back to Termon, although there's nothing much there for me except a butler's life on fourteen shillings a week."

"And Feedo."

"Ah yes. I love the way you say Fido."

She leaned over him, her face serious, as she waved a buttercup over his nose.

"Will you take me home to meet him? And walk with you in the Glen?"

"If you like. Although you'd find Tyrone very cold and damp compared with here."

She tickled his nose with the buttercup.

"You could always come here and live with me. We could have seventeen children and swim naked in the river every morning."

"You know, that might not be such a bad idea. We could call them all Junior to avoid confusion. Especially the girls."

She did not answer, and he looked up.

"But then, maybe you are right about thinking so far. I have these terrible feelings sometimes, that something dreadful is going to happen," she said.

"Yes. But then, there's no point in worrying. All worrying does is make you worried. Better to enjoy the day that's in it. Carpe diem."

"Ah yes. Seize the fish," she laughed.

"Come on, then. Let's seize the fish and have a swim before our seventeen children wake up."

She looked down at him, her gloom dispelled.

"Good idea," she said, starting to unbutton his shirt. "But there's no point getting clean without getting dirty first."

"You're so cheeky," said Max. "I can't think of a single thing I like about you."

She kissed his chest.

"Not even one?"

"Not one."

She began to unbutton his trousers.

"Well, maybe just one."

He loved so many things about Yvette, as he looked at her lying asleep in the sun after their swim.

Even if deep in his heart there was buried a feeling that had its roots back in Termon, and which was such a tender and exquisite longing that he dared not sully it with a name.

But then, there was no point in thinking of things he could do nothing about, any more than there was thinking about the future.

* * *

"Do you think you'll ever settle down, chum? I mean, fall in love and get married, and all that if we get through this Godawful business?" he said to Bentley over hot pot and a bottle of average Burgundy in the mess that evening.

"Me? I suppose if I survive it I'll go back to Cambridge, finish the law degree and end up with a bored wife, two spoilt brats and a black Labrador," said Bentley, then looked gloomily into his glass.

"But there's not much point in thinking about any of that when we might be dead tomorrow, is there? I mean, look at Smyth. One minute happily sailing along fretting about his perfect formation, the next thing a million charred molecules proceeding to earth. Presumably in formation."

"Yes. I was just saying the same thing to Yvette earlier. Or maybe she was to me."

"She's a peach. I think you should marry her. As for me, I think I'm more in love with falling in love than with being in love. And besides, with an unlimited supply of lovely nurses, who wants to settle down?"

"Good point," laughed Max, pouring him another glass. "You know, the only good thing about this wine is that it makes you appreciate the stuff in Jack's."

It rained all the next morning, so he spent it working on his engine, which was running slightly rough, then took it up for a test before lunch in a clearing sky.

He was circling back to land when he looked down and saw, to his amazement, a yellow and lilac Albatros with a red spinner cruising over the field as if the pilot hadn't a care in the world.

"Someone's feeling particularly suicidal," he said, then sideslipped until he was only 50 yards above and behind it. He cocked his guns, then gave them a one-second burst.

The Albatros jumped as if in alarm, and the pilot looked around. Seeing that there was no escape, he hunched down in his cockpit as if waiting for the hail of bullets.

Max slid alongside, and pointed down at the field. The German nodded, then slid down to an uneventful landing.

Max landed, taxied up, and walked over.

"Sind Sie ziemlich verrückt?" he said, as the pilot removed his helmet to reveal a shock of blond hair and a handsome, youthful face.

"Yes, I must be," he said in slightly accented English. "I made a bet with the other fellows at dinner last night that it would be quite safe to fly over your field at lunchtime, because the English will never go flying on an empty stomach."

"I thought that was the French," laughed Max, glancing at his watch as two mechanics came running over with Lee Enfields. "Well, the bad news is you're a prisoner of war. The good news is you're just in time for lunch, and it's roast beef and Yorkshire pudding."

"Of course. That makes up for everything," said the German pilot with a wan smile, holding out his hand. "Vizefeldwebel Hans Zimmerman."

"Delighted. Max Edwards. Lieutenant," said Max. "You may as well stay for dinner as well, and we'll hand you over in the morning."

"So which Jagdstaffel are you with?" said Uncle that evening after Zimmerman's third glass of wine.

"I don't think I am allowed to say," said Zimmerman.

"Well, you may as well tell us," said Max. "They'll torture it out of you back in Blighty."

"Torture?"

"Absolutely. We've heard some terrible stories. Makes my hair curl," said Bentley.

"Foot tickling. Chinese burns. Listening to Bentley's jokes, that sort of thing," said Max.

Zimmerman looked at them both, then smiled.

"Ha! You are joking. Well, I suppose it makes no difference. Jasta 14."

"Ah? Voss' outfit. I've run into him. What's he like?" said Max.

"Brilliant flyer, but a bit of a strange fellow. Likes to fly on his own. Son of a dyer, but in spite of that, gets on very well with von Richthofen, who is, as you know, a Prussian nobleman.

"Some of the fellows frown on the way he calls his mechanics by their first names. He actually enjoys working on his machine with them, wearing this dirty jacket with no insignia, although in the air he always wears a silk shirt and scarf."

"Good thing too," said Bentley. "Stops your neck rubbing when you're searching the sky for nasty chaps who want to shoot you down. Like you, for example."

"And you," laughed Zimmerman, "although he says the reason is that if he's captured he wants to be presentable to the girls in Paris. Loves his motorcycle, as well."

"Looks like you've got a kindred spirit, Max," said Bentley.

"Quite," said the CO. "One's got a Blue Max, and the other was a blue Max when he landed after his first flight."

"Good God," said Uncle. "I do believe our leader has cracked a joke."

Max and Bentley put a merry Zimmerman to bed at one am, then looked at him lying there snoring gently.

"He's just the same as us," said Bentley. "What on earth is the point of this all?"

"Good question," said Max. "If you find out, do let me know."

The next morning, they stood with Zimmerman watching a Crossley tender rumble up to take him away.

"Oh well. Thank you for your hospitality. Perhaps I will return the favour one day," he said.

"I look forward to it," said Max.

"Oh, just one thing. Since I lost the bet about you fellows all being at lunch, perhaps you would be good enough to drop this cheque at my field."

He handed it over, and Max put it in his pocket.

"Of course. I'll make sure I do it at lunchtime."

Hans laughed, shook their hands, and after a last forlorn look at his Albatros, climbed into the back of the tender.

"What the —" said Max, sitting up in bed with a jerk as the rattle of machinegun fire woke him.

Beside him, Bentley was already out of bed, and they flung open the door of the hut to see a pair of Albatri disappear over the hedge in the grey light of dawn, leaving behind it a pair of Nieuports which were already well ablaze, giving the field an eerie glow in which Max saw something white lying in the grass.

He walked over, and picked it up. It was a sheet of paper, weighted with a stone and tied with a red ribbon.

He opened it and read: "Do give our regards to Vizefeldwebel Zimmerman, and ask him if he would be so kind as to pay his gambling debts. Our very best regards, Jasta 14, Marchais."

"Cheeky buggers," said Bentley, standing beside him. "I was having this dream that I was being machine-gunned to death, and woke to find it was all too true. What are you going to do?"

"Exactly what they say, of course," said Max. "I'll just go and get Fred to load us up with some Cooper bombs."

The next morning, just after dawn, two Pups fell from the sky over Marchais airfield and swept towards a row of twelve Albatros DVs lined up with inch-perfect precision

"Germans. They're so tidy," said Max, as he and Bentley raced along the row with their bombs falling away and machineguns clattering.

As he passed the last one, he took the envelope containing Zimmerman's cheque out of his pocket, attached to a red streamer, and dropped it over the side of the cockpit, then as they rose over the hedge with bullets from the perimeter defences sailing over their heads, looked back to see several of the Albatri ablaze, and two bouncing across the grass.

He and Bentley tore back across the field. He caught the one on the left with a three-second burst, saw it stagger and crash into a hedge, then looked over to see the one Bentley was firing at fly at full speed through the open doors of a hangar.

For a moment, the roar of its engine echoed around the hangar, then there was a mighty explosion, and flames and smoke mushroomed out.

Bentley's Pup popped out of the inferno a second later, and they put their noses down and raced for home at zero feet, roaring flat out across the German trenches before the surprised troops below had a chance to fire.

"Strewth, that was a bit of rare excitement," said Bentley over bacon and eggs back at Maranique. "That's the last we'll see of that lot, I hope."

"I wouldn't bet on it," said Max. "I think an early start is called for tomorrow."

The next morning, a solitary insomniac cockerel was the only sound to be heard in the darkness before the dawn.

Bentley shivered, peered over the edge of the sandbag, and wiped the dew off the Vickers with his handkerchief.

"Not a peep," he said, then cocked an ear. "Ah, but hark."

From the west came the sweet purr of a Mercedes engine, which changed to an angry growl as a yellow Albatros with a red lightning flash along its side swept over their heads, and a bright red sphere with streamers attached fell from it and bounced across the grass and came to rest ten yards from them.

"What the hell is it?" said Max.

"Some kind of new secret weapon. Give it a rattle."

Max put a five-second burst into the red object. Nothing happened. Suspecting a trick, he got up and walked towards it, followed by Bentley.

There was a strange whispering sound coming from it, and for a moment Max wondered if it was some sort of delayed action fuse.

Then he bent over, laughed, and gave it a kick.

“It’s a bloody football. What a bunch of jokers,” he said.

Chapter Sixteen

August 1917

"Well, what do you think?" said Bentley as Max jumped down from the first of the new Camels the Squadron was getting to replace the Pups.

"I think Tommy Sopwith is either a madman or a genius," said Max, "and I haven't decided which. I tried a gentle turn to the right, and the nose dropped like a stone. Then I tried a gentle turn to the left, and it reared like a bucking bronco.

"I gave up turning after that, and tried just flying straight and level. Won't do it. Elevator's like a hair trigger, rudder's useless, and you need to shove the stick forward all the time because it's so tail heavy. I let go for a moment just to see what happened, and it headed for heaven like a homesick angel, then flicked into a spin."

"They all do that, sir," said Fred, who'd wandered up wiping his hands on an oily rag. Possibly the same one he'd had since the start of the war.

"Now where have I heard that before?" said Max.

"Maybe Sopwith made it deliberately unstable for jinking, since we never fly straight and level anyway," said Bentley.

"Maybe so. Still, at least that new Constantinesco synchronizer works, even with the twin Vickers. I waited until I was over the airfield before I gave it a rattle, but the prop's still on. Fancy a go?"

Half an hour later, Bentley landed, got out and mopped his brow.

"Jesus. Pirouettes like a ballerina I went out with in London once. Jessica. Lovely girl. Used to dance for me wearing nothing but her pointes."

He sighed at the memory, then patted the hump of the Camel approvingly.

"Climbs like a bandit with 130 horses on board, mind you, and flick rolls are a hoot. Hark, there's Hobson."

They turned to look as a Bristol Fighter from 169 Squadron based at St Omer Nord came sliding in to land with a silky growl from its Rolls-Royce Falcon.

"Hello, chaps," said Hobson. "This one of your shiny new Camels? What's she like to fly?"

"Piece of cake," said Max. "You can just tootle around the sky all day long reading a good book while it flies itself."

Hobson looked at him suspiciously.

"That's not what I've heard," he said.

"Why don't you find out for yourself?" said Bentley. "We'll swap you for a ride in your Brisfit."

"All right then. How hard can it be?" said Hobson.

Max tossed a coin with Bentley, then climbed into the front seat of the Bristol with Bentley in the rear, and they watched as Fred swung the Camel's prop and Hobson swung it into wind then sailed jerkily into the sky.

Max looked around to see Bentley crossing himself, and laughed.

"Come on, let's give this Biff a twirl," he said.

He threw it around the sky for half an hour, and was circling back over the airfield to land when he suddenly had an idea.

He looked back at Bentley and twirled his forefinger. Bentley looked at him blankly, then grinned and nodded.

Max undid his safety belt, stood up on the wicker pilot's seat, then turned around, planted one leg on the observer's rotating stool and grabbed the Scarff ring on which were mounted the twin Vickers.

Bentley, meanwhile, had done the same, and they climbed past each other, wobbled for one teetering moment, and got themselves settled into their new positions.

From the back seat, Max clapped Bentley on the shoulder. His friend turned around, clasped his hand, and they laughed as one at the glorious lunacy of it all.

"Lovely. Rolling takes a bit of a shove, but she's pretty splitarse for a big bird, isn't she?" said Bentley as they taxied back in and switched off just in time to see Hobson come in to land, bounce twice, then switch off and climb shakily out of the Camel.

He walked over, his face like thunder, then laughed when he saw the grins on their faces.

"Bastards," he said, then hugged the fuselage of the Bristol.

"I love you, Bob. I'll never leave you again," he said, and they all laughed, then Hobson stood back and looked at each of them in turn.

"Hang on. Weren't you…or…or…am I losing my mind again?" he said.

"It's all right," said Bentley. "We've stayed in the same positions. We just turned the aeroplane around."

That afternoon was glorious, with gold and tawny clouds tumbling all over the sky, and Max took the Camel up again, dancing it about the sky and getting to like it more and more.

Apart from a distant barrage balloon, there was nothing else to be seen, for these days all the Huns stooged around in packs protecting each other's tails, apart from a few lone wolves who still hunted alone.

He flew along humming Schubert's Trout Quintet to himself, then looked down to see a vast canyon of clear blue air between two soaring cirrocumulus the colour of buttermilk.

Tipping the Camel on its edge, he threw the aircraft into it, spiralling and laughing, then plunged into the wall of white and began climbing through the ethereal murk.

Apart from the roar of the engine, there was no sensation of movement apart from the chill droplets of moisture on his goggles. It was eerie, as if he and the Camel had become an airborne version of the Mary Celeste, and he shivered, not at the chill, but at the thought that he had suddenly become a ghost without any warning.

A minute went by, then as suddenly as he had entered the cloud, he popped out into bright sunlight.

And gasped as the tail of an Albatros appeared right in front of the Camel's nose.

He kicked hard on the rudder bar and slid alongside, his wingtip missing the Albatros' by inches, then looked over to see a red heart and a laurel wreath.

Voss looked across, startled, then recognised him, pushed his goggles up, and saluted.

"You look older and wearier than the first time we met, chum," said Max. "But you'd probably say the same about me."

He made a motion of wiping sweat off his brow, and Voss threw back his head and laughed, then nodded.

Uncertain what to do, they flew along side by side for a bit, and then Voss looked up and around to check the sky was clear.

Then he reached forward, cocked the safety lock on the back of each Spandau, looked across and made a swooping and diving motion with his free hand.

Max looked at him blankly, then it dawned on him.

"I don't believe it. He wants to play," said Max.

He reached forward to the wishbone-shaped safety catches on the Vickers, then nodded, and dived away. In his mirror he saw Voss dive after him.

He glanced in his rear view mirror and saw the red spinner of the Albatros slide into position only yards behind his tail, then flick-rolled the Camel to the left and glanced in his mirror again.

The red spinner was still there, as if it never moved.

"Brilliant," laughed Max. "Bloody brilliant."

After ten minutes of failing to shake Voss off his tail, he reached up and made a rotating motion with his hand. The red spinner vanished, and Voss slid in front of the Camel.

Max managed to stay on his tail, but only just. His nerves taut with concentration, he glanced down at his instrument panel, then pulled out of the chase.

Voss looked over his shoulder, then throttled back and slid alongside. Max pointed to his fuel tank.

Voss nodded, then made a fist and tapped it twice on his chest above his heart.

Max saluted him, then tilted away.

What a strange encounter, he thought as he turned for home. What a strange chap. What a bloody marvellous pilot.

"Don't tell a soul," he said to Bentley in Jack's that night, "but you're never going to believe what happened to me today."

Chapter Seventeen

September 1917

The mist was just burning off the field to reveal a glorious early autumn day, and Max was climbing into his flying suit when he looked up to see a Nieuport coming in.

It stopped, and Mannock climbed out and came walking over.

"Hello, Edward. I see you're officially an ace," said Max.

"Bollocks to that," said Mannock. "It just means I saw six Fritzes before they saw me. Two of them were real flamerinoes."

He made a downward curving machine with his left hand.

"Sizzle sizzle wonk. Oh, I see we got Voss the boy wonder."

"What? When?"

"Just yesterday, over Poelkapelle. Hell of a scrap, by all accounts. Apparently he took on 60 Squadron and chased them off, then got into a tangle with half a dozen S.E.5s from 56."

"Ah yes, McCudden, Rhys Davids and that bunch," said Bentley.

"That's the one, so. He'd changed from the Albatros to that new Tripehound of his with the funny face on the front, so he out-climbed them and could have got away, then just turned and came back at them again. Actually hit all of them. Rhys Davids got him in the end."

"Any chance he survived?" said Max.

"Not a hope. I was over there last night, and Mac said the Tripe went straight in and disappeared in a thousand pieces. He seemed quite cut up about it.

"They actually drank a toast to the bugger in the mess last night. Hang on. I wrote it down, because I couldn't believe it."

He fumbled in his pocket, and fished out a scrap of paper.

"Here we are. 'His flying was wonderful, his courage magnificent, and in my opinion he was the bravest German airman whom it has been my privilege to see fight.'

"That was Mac. And Rhys Davids was wandering around muttering that he wished he'd brought him down alive."

"I know what they mean. I feel like I've lost a friend, or something," said Max.

"Don't be a silly bastard. Just one less Fritz for us to worry about, as far as I'm concerned," said Mannock.

"Yes, there is that," said Bentley. "You staying for a gargle?"

"Don't mind if I do, so," said Mannock, as the CO came walking over.

"Hello, Mannock. Edwards, congratulations. You've just been made Captain."

"Well done, chum," said Bentley, shaking his hand. "I remember the day when you could barely tie your own shoelaces, and now look at you. A fully paid up member of the ruling classes."

"Sounds like time for a double gargle, so," said Mannock, as Max sat there, half in and half out of his flying suit, wondering which side he was on.

September 1917, a week later

"Edwards, this is Jones," said the CO. "Try to keep him alive. Jones, this is Captain Edwards. He'll be your Flight Commander."

Max turned to find an attenuated teenager leaping to his feet with a toothy grin and an extended hand.

"Very pleased to meet you, sir. Gosh, I can't wait to get out there and get a crack at the Hun."

"Don't be too eager, Jones," said Max. "The Hun's just as eager to get a crack at you. Let me introduce you to Lieutenant Priory and Sergeant Rogerson and get you a kite sorted, then we'll take you up and show you the ropes tomorrow."

"Gosh. Great. Flying is such terrific fun, isn't it?" said Jones.

"Any advice, sir?" said Jones as they stood in front of his Camel the next morning. It was, of course, the worst in the squadron, but Max had at least made sure it flew more or less straight, and that the engine was sound and the guns true.

"Yes. Always attack with the advantages of height and speed," said Max. "For scouts, get in as close as you can. Otherwise you're just wasting His Majesty's precious bullets. For two-seaters, you can get under them as close as you can where the observer can't get at you, then pull the stick back and let them have it.

"And never, ever stop scanning the sky for Huns. Especially in the sun," said Bentley.

"What if I get one on my tail, sir?"

"Pray. And keep jinking. Kick the rudder bar and skid sideways. It takes a good pilot to hit a skidding Camel. If you cut the throttle at the same time, he may whizz past you and you can get on his tail. Otherwise, a half roll then a half loop's very good for getting back and coming at them," said Max.

"Oh, and it used to be that we could out-turn them in a circle, but not with these new Fokker triplanes. And you'll find out for yourself, but the Camel's a skittish beast. When you turn left, the nose always pitches up," said Bentley.

"And drops when you turn right, so you'll need buckets of top rudder," said Max.

"Yes, sir. Gyroscopic effect of the rotary engine, small rudder and all that."

"Clever boy," said Max. "Right, let's go up and do some dogfighting. First of all, I'll be a Hun and you have to chase me, then I'll return the favour. If I get bored or you accidentally ram me, Bentley will take over."

"Right-o," said Jones.

An hour of dancing around the sky later, they landed and switched off.

"He's bloody good," said Bentley.

"Bloody good," said Max as Jones came bounding over.

"Gosh, that was fun. How did I do?"

"Oh, not too bad," said Bentley, then laughed out loud at Jones' crestfallen face.

"I like you, Jonesie," said Max, slapping Jones on the back. "I think you'll do very well. Very well indeed."

"Gosh, sir, thank you. Thank you very much," beamed Jones.

"My pleasure. Now go and get some sleep. Across the Lines tomorrow to show you your way around."

"Gosh. Can't wait. I mean in a half scared, half excited, half giddy sort of way."

"That's three halves, but never mind. Off you go," said Max as a staff car came rolling across the field and a Major got out.

"Gosh, hello, Dad!" said Jones, then blushed. "Sorry, I mean sir."

"That's all right, chum," said the Major.

"This is Edwards and Priory, sir. They've got 28 and 27 Huns on the blackboard in the mess. They've been showing me the ropes, and we're going across the Lines tomorrow. I'm terribly excited," said Jones.

"How do you do," said the Major, shaking their hands. "You will take care of him, won't you? He's all we have."

"I think he'll do very well, sir," said Max. "Very well indeed."

"Gosh," said Jones. "Thank you, sir."

As Max climbed into bed that night, he was trying for the life of him to think who Jones reminded him of.

And then, on the edge of sleep, it came to him.

Fido. He smiled, rolled over, and pulled the scratchy blankets up to his chin.

The next morning, they were at 15,000 ft when Max saw the Rumpler 5,000 ft below and about three miles ahead.

As they crawled closer, he could see that the pilot was looking straight ahead, and the observer was peering over the side.

"Mmm, looks a bit fishy," he muttered, and holding his thumb over the sun, scanned the sky above for any sign of enemy scouts waiting for someone to hook the decoy. But there was only a single cloud, proceeding west in a stately fashion.

He looked across at Bentley and jerked his thumb at Jones. Bentley nodded, and Max looked over at Jones, waggled his wings and pointed to the Rumpler, but he had already seen it.

"Good boy," said Max. "Sharp as a tack."

With his hand, Max made a swooping movement to remind Jones to get underneath it, then gave him a thumbs up. Jonesie grinned, and dived away.

"An easy first kill. Please God," said Max, as Jones closed in and slid under the two-seater.

And then, some buried instinct made Max glance up. Just in time to see an unholy trinity of triplanes hurtling down out of the single cloud.

"Bastards," he said, as the all-red leader shot past him and Bentley, followed by the rest. It was Jones they were after.

"Richthofen! Oh shit, oh shit, oh shit," said Max, pushing the throttle wide open and diving after them, followed by Bentley.

They closed on the last two and with a brief salvo send them spiralling away, but it was too late. Max watched in despair as Richthofen closed.

"Just a few seconds more, Jonesie," he said grimly, his jaw clenched.

At the last minute, Jones glanced over his shoulder and saw the red triplane bearing down him. Just as Richthofen stitched the Camel with a row of bullets.

Jones soared to the right, and for a moment it looked as if he had got away with it. Then a stream of white vapour began to pour back from his engine.

"No. Please no," said Max, as a lick of flame appeared, then grew until it engulfed the cockpit.

Jones stood up, wreathed in flames, and jumped. Max watched in horror as he fell, tumbling over and over, followed by the spiralling inferno of his Camel.

It finally disappeared from sight, leaving behind a corkscrew of black smoke, and Max slumped in his seat, then looked up. Bentley was chasing after Richthofen, but had no hope of catching him, and to the east, the Rumpler had its nose down and was a distant speck.

Max shoved the throttle forward and sped after it. He knew he was getting deeper into enemy territory, and low on fuel, but he didn't care.

Ten minutes later, he rose underneath it, gave it a five-second burst from stem to stern, and watched as it fell to earth, slowly at first then faster and faster, until the top wing folded back and went fluttering down to earth like a sycamore leaf.

He ran out of fuel as he curved in to land back at Maranique and glided in, then sat in the cockpit for a minute to compose himself and get the image of Jones burning out of his head.

"I choose to forget," he said to himself as Sergeant Rogerson came trotting up.

"You all right, sir?" said Fred.

"Quite, Fred."

"Jones not back, sir?"

"Afraid not. Flamer."

"Oh dear," said Fred as Bentley walked up.

"I think we need to go out and get very drunk," he said. "Immediately."

Half an hour later, they were sitting in Jack's with a bottle of Gevrey-Chambertin in front of them and Vivienne, Bentley's latest conquest, beside them.

Another nurse from his unlimited supply, she was from the little village of Yalding in Kent, and in spite of the mud and blood surrounding them, bore with her the scent of rosewater and the summer fields of her home.

"Ah, Chambertin," said Max. "The wine of which Victor Hugo said: 'I cannot remember the town, and the name of the girl escapes me, but the wine was Chambertin'."

"Can't believe he forgot the name of the girl," said Bentley, pouring another glass. "Bollocks and buggery. Vivienne, this stuff must be evaporating in the heat of your unremitting passion for me. Be a dear and get us another one."

"You two should settle the war by a drinking game with the Germans. Then it would be over by Christmas," said Vivienne, rising and threading her way silkily to the bar.

"Talking of buggery, she's strangely attracted to it. Surprising, in such an English rose," said Bentley when she was out of earshot. "Or is it sodomy?"

"It's buggery. Sodomy is between chaps," said Max.

"Can't see the attraction myself," said Bentley, "although apparently it's compulsory in the Navy. First time I've done it, either way. Strangely fascinating. The old boy makes a strange pop when he retreats from the heat of battle. Can't decide whether it's a sound or a sensation."

"You are disgusting, Bentley," said Max as Vivienne returned and planted her sweetly buggered bottom on the bench beside Bentley.

"What have you two been talking about?" she said.

"Pre-Raphaelite poetry," said Bentley. "Nothing like a good Rossetti to nod off to of an evening."

"Indeed. Sleep is a goodly thing, before the daybreak hours that onward creep. Or something. I'm drunk," said Max.

"Not drunk enough," said Bentley, pouring them all another glass.

The next morning, he woke at dawn with a hammering head to see the blessed relief of rain and low cloud, and fell asleep again, walking to the mess at nine to find Bentley and the CO tucking into bacon and eggs.

"Best order tonight, you two. We've got a visitor from Farnborough HQ this evening. Colonel Basildon-ffrench. Here to perk us all up."

"Bully for him," said Max. "Any bacon left?"

That night, they all filed into the crowded mess to find the CO and the portly figure of Basildon-ffrench.

"Good evening, gentlemen," he said. "I am here to tell you that the war is going well, and Trenchard is very pleased with you all.

"He wants you all to continue with Distant Offensive Patrols and hit the Hun where it hurts. If our Teutonic friends know that we can reach deep into their territory and strike them on their own airfields, we are winning the battle in the air, which is every bit as important as the battle in the trenches. Although just don't tell the Poor Bloody Infantry that."

He paused, waiting for laughter, and a stern look from Major Cunningham forced a chuckle.

"Right, any questions before dinner?" said the CO.

Bentley put his hand up.

"Sir, yesterday we all watched a promising new boy, Jones, jump from his flaming kite and burn to death all the way down from 16,000 ft. On our side of No Man's Land. If he'd had a parachute, the dear boy would be sitting with us this evening. Why can't we have them?"

"Too new-fangled, I'm afraid. They haven't been tried and tested properly, for a start," said Basildon-ffrench.

"I'm afraid that's not true. Sir. They were dreamed of back in the 15th Century, da Vinci drew one, Garnerin demonstrated a rigid one in…"

"1797," said Max.

"Thank you, Max. Blanchard made the first compact one from folded silk, Berry jumped from an aircraft using one in 1912, and with Van Meter's ripcord device, we could open them when we're well away from a burning aircraft."

"Fascinating history lesson, gentlemen," said Basildon-ffrench. "Unfortunately, they might be all right for balloonists, but they're too bulky to fit into a cockpit."

"Bit like yourself," muttered Max, loud enough for everyone around him to hear.

"What was that?" said Basildon-ffrench.

"He said he thinks it's going to rain later," said Bentley.

"Quite. Well, as I say, they're not suitable for scouts," said Basildon-ffrench when the ripple of laughter had died down.

"With all due respect, sir, that's not the case. Calthrop's Guardian Angel design was tested by Collett earlier this year from the cockpit of a B.E.2.c," said Bentley.

"That's as may be. The Air Board looked at Collett's design, and decided there was no point to it, since most accidents happen on takeoff and landing.

"In any case, the powers that be — including me, I must say — feel that if our chaps had parachutes, it might impair the fighting spirit. Men would jump out rather than fight on, or abandon machines which could otherwise be brought back for repair."

There was silence as everyone in the room looked at him, the air thick with loathing.

"Have you ever been in combat, sir?" said Bentley.

"That's enough, Priory," said the CO, looking at his pocket watch. "Time for dinner. The carrots will be ruined."

Dinner was a quiet affair. Basildon-ffrench left before pudding.

"Shame. He missed an excellent crumble," said Bentley.

The next day, they'd just returned from an uneventful dawn patrol when a Crossley tender rumbled up and discharged a corporal carrying a small wooden box. He saluted the CO.

"Beg pardon, sir. Your man Jones. Or what's left of him. Sign here, if you would."

They buried the box that afternoon, under a generous oak in the local cemetery.

"Tell me, chaplain, do you ever see a conflict between what you do and the sixth commandment?" said Max as they walked back from the cemetery. "I mean, it doesn't exactly come with footnotes excluding Huns, Italians, Boers, Mesopotamians or whoever we happen to be at war with at that particular moment. Especially since the Huns are probably convinced that God wears a pickelhaube."

The chaplain stopped, and looked up at the scudding clouds.

"Every day, to be honest. I suppose I think my role here is to provide consolation for those who feel they are fighting a just war."

He paused.

"And possibly even more succour to those who feel there is no such thing. And you?"

"The war? The war's a load of bollocks. Not just because a Serbian shot an Austrian, but because of the alliance between Germany, Austria-Hungary and Italy thirty years ago.

"Once Britain, France, and Russia formed their own little gang against that, Europe was just two armed camps bristling with gung-ho nationalism, imperialism and militarism. It only took the spark of Princep's gun to set them at each other's throats.

"And as for religion, I'm an atheist, thank God. No offence."

"None taken," said the chaplain. "God still loves you."

"Good old God," said Max, as the rain started.

That night, he was sitting in the mess glumly reading the Wipers Times as the rain lashed the windows with a vengeance when the door swung open and Bentley staggered in carrying a large gramophone, followed by Uncle with a wooden box which he was trying to protect from the weather with his coat.

"Whose is that?" said Max.

"Jonesie's. Bloody good one too, by the looks of things. May as well get some use out of it," said Bentley, setting it down on a corner table.

Max got up, walked over and bent down to inspect the brass maker's plaque on the side.

"Berliner. Bloody unpatriotic," he said, taking out his clasp knife and prising the offending plaque out as Uncle picked a record from the box, put it on and prepared to swing the needle down.

"Wait," said Bentley. "We need to christen the Jonesie Memorial Gramophone."

He went to the bar and brought back a bottle of Moët.

"I prefer Bollinger, but this will have to do," he said, pouring three glasses as the CO came in and shook the rain off his hat.

"Just in time, sir. Grab a glass and join us," said Bentley.

They raised their glasses and saluted the gramophone.

"A toast," said Bentley. "To the Jonesie Memorial Gramophone," then Uncle swung the needle down and the record crackled and hissed into life with the opening notes of a piano concerto.

"Is that Grieg?" said Max, after a few bars.

Uncle made a pantomime of moving his head around and around to check the rotating label, then fell against a laughing Bentley, pretending to be giddy

"That champers has gone right to my head. It is. Good spot."

Max sighed, and returned to his seat and the Wipers Times, his fingers unconsciously slipping into his pocket and gently touching the carp.

He finished the Times, left it on a side table, and went to the window. On the horizon, the guns thundered and flickered on the front, which was a couple of miles further on than last year. Or was it a couple of miles further back. He could never remember.

As he stood there looking through the rain-lashed window, with the light and music and banter of the mess behind him and the flickering darkness in front, he felt as if he was back again standing at the French windows in the drawing room at Termon on the night of the ball, looking at little Annie Jameson falling and falling forever from the giant oak.

Or perhaps it was Kumiko, falling from her father's arms.

Falling, he thought. Everyone was falling, except out here there was no soft grass or passing neighbour to catch you.

Oh well. At least there was Yvette. And Bentley.

Max looked up through the window at the night sky as thunder rumbled and a flash of lightning split the sky, echoing the barrage as it had the night he'd ridden home from Amiens with Yvette that first night.

Keep them safe, God, he thought. *Let them not fall.*

Then he remembered that God was possibly German.

"Max! What are you doing over there?" came the voice of Uncle.

"Speaking to God. In German," said Max.

"Well, tell him it's his round," said Bentley.

It rained solidly for nine days, and on the following Thursday, he and Bentley huddled in the fug of Jack's, sharing a bottle of Beaujolais Villages.

A slim brunette walked through the door, saw Bentley, waved and came over.

"Joanne," said Bentley, waving the bottle. "Like a drink?"

"I'll get a glass," said Joanne, making her way to the bar.

"What happened to Vivienne?" said Max.

"Vivienne is Tuesdays. Joanne is Thursdays," said Bentley. "Lovely girl. Black belt in the dark art of oral delights. Uses the same technique as starting a Camel. Contact. Suck in. Ignition."

"Help," said Max, as Joanne returned, and held out her glass for Bentley to fill.

"Bloody hell, that bottle didn't last long," he said, then looked at the bar to find that Pierre had vanished.

"I'll just have to help myself," he said to Max. "Keep me covered, and I'll pass a bottle over to you. I hope to see my pilot face to face, when I have crossed the bar."

"Tennyson. Very good, Bentley. You're more civilised than you claim to be," said Max.

"Public school, chum. Damned good thrashing once a day and twice on Sundays, cold showers, terrible grub, rugby on Wednesdays and Tennyson on Fridays, courtesy of Master Henderson when he wasn't feeling up the fags," said Bentley as they reached the bar. "Ah, here's Pierre back. Mission abandoned. Stand down all hands."

Chapter Eighteen

March 1918

"I don't know about you, chum, but this endless ground strafing is getting to me," said Bentley. "I mean, it's one thing being up there in the burning blue with Richthofen and Co chasing you round and round like blue-arsed flies, but quite another being a target for every Tom, Dick and Hans in the German trenches to take pot shots at."

"We're not the only ones who are worn out," said Max, nodding to where Fred, Blythe and Evans were patching a Camel back together again. "They've been at that all night. And the night before."

He looked up to see the CO walking towards them in the grey light of dawn, leaving a trail of footsteps in the dewy grass.

"Any news, sir?" said Max.

"Nothing fresh, really. Haig says this big push by the Huns is the greatest crisis of the war. Worst losses on our side since the Somme, but apparently our strafing is the only thing keeping Jerry's head down. Just got this from Salmond at Field HQ to all squadrons."

He took a slip of paper from his pocket and read it out.

"Squadrons will bomb and shoot up everything they can see on the enemy side of the line west of Bapaume. Very low flying is essential. All risks to be taken. Urgent."

"Not sure how much lower he wants," said Bentley. "I actually knocked the pickelhaube off a cavalry officer yesterday with my left wheel. And he wasn't even on his horse."

They climbed wearily into their machines, did four patrols that day, landed at dark, had a brief bite, and fell straight into bed.

Johnston woke them at 7.30 am with two mugs of tea.

"Dud, sir," he said, jerking his head upwards to the steady patter of rain on the roof of the hut.

"Hurrah. Pop over to the mess and order breakfast for eleven o'clock," said Max.

As Johnston opened and closed the door on his way out, Max caught a brief glimpse of low cloud and sheets of rain sweeping across the airfield.

"Bliss," said Bentley, then fell back asleep, his tea untouched.

Max finished his tea, and had just nodded off when the door opened. It was Cunningham.

"Get into flying kit, chaps," he said, taking off his cap and shaking the rain off it.

"You are joking, sir. Tell me you're having a laugh," said Bentley.

"Sorry. Orders from Wing," said the CO, then put on his sodden cap and closed the door.

Climbing away from the field, they hit cloud almost immediately, and crawled towards the Lines.

The rain pricked Max's face like a thousand tiny needles, and blinded him as it slashed across his goggles. He pushed them up, but that was even worse, so he pulled them back down again.

They passed over a battery of 60-pounders firing across the river, and their Camels bucked and weaved in the turbulence of the passing shells.

The battery was firing at Huns on the other side of the river as they tried to cross the bridge and take Villers-Bretonneux, and Max stuck his nose down and flew along it at fifty feet strafing them, followed by Bentley.

A constant stream of tracers from the German machineguns on the far side rose to greet them, and Max ducked as a neat group of holes appeared in the centre section above his head, then laughed at the uselessness of ducking.

They soared across the far bank, rose into the murk, half-rolled and came back at the bridge in a hail of bullets.

This is suicidal, thought Max. It's only a matter of time before we go west.

Their Vickers chattered, and to his intense relief, he saw khaki figures stream across the bridge and launch into the Germans. There was no point firing on them now.

They stooged up and down the Lines, firing on random machine gun nests until they ran out of ammunition, then went home, had breakfast and watched as the cloud descended until it was brushing the treetops.

"Bloody hell," said Rogerson when he saw the state of their aircraft. "Flying patchwork quilts. Blythe!"

"Sir?"

"Get your needlework kit out. We've some sewing to do."

At lunchtime, the CO appeared.

"Good show this morning. Not much more we can do at low level, so could be a washout for the rest of the day," he said.

They went to bed for an hour, then were awakened again by the CO.

"Sorry, another show. It's lifted a bit," he said.

They flew back to the bridge, where the British troops on it waved at them, then flew up and down the Lines, which as far as they could tell underneath the inferno of smoke and flame, were holding against the German push.

After an hour, Max looked up and saw a patch of blue sky which was almost big enough to make a sailor suit, waggled his wings and pointed.

Bentley looked across, gave a thumbs up, and they rose together into the glorious clear blue air and sunshine above the clouds and hell below.

It looked clear to the German side, and they climbed to 17,000 ft and sailed about for a bit, then spotted a brace of Triplanes about 5,000 ft below and dived on them, the wind screaming through the wires and the airspeed indicator nudging 160, but the rear Hun must have looked up and seen them coming, because when they were still far out of range, the Tripes put their noses down and dived for home.

Huns never wanted to fight these days. All the experienced ones flew around in giant circuses like the Richthofen mob, and the rest were youngsters who got in a funk the moment they saw a Camel and went running for home.

Max levelled out, and the engine coughed. He looked down to see that the pressure had dropped, and pumped the handle, but nothing happened. The valve on the fuel pump must have blown with the dive. He switched over to the gravity tank, and the engine picked up again, then looked over at Bentley.

Except Bentley was not there.

Max tilted the Camel on its side and looked down the wing at the earth below. Ah, there he was, gliding down with his propeller stopped.

Max eased back the power and slid down alongside him with a questioning look, and Bentley shrugged his shoulders, then looked down to see if there was somewhere to land.

He slid neatly over a copse and into a meadow, then climbed out and waved, and Max looked up and around to make sure the Triplanes hadn't returned, then landed and taxied up.

"What is it?" he shouted over the urgent putter of the idling Le Rhone.

"Out of petrol. I think ground fire must have nicked the fuel line," said Bentley.

"OK. Don't go away. I'll be back," said Max, then swung the Camel into wind and was gone.

Half an hour later, he landed at St Omer Nord and jumped out as Hobson came walking over.

"Hello, Edwards. What's up?"

"Bentley's down about ten miles into Hunland. Any chance of borrowing a Brisfit to pick him up?"

Max retraced his route, and breathed a sigh of relief when he saw Bentley standing beside his Camel.

As Max taxied the Bristol Fighter in, he saw Bentley reach into the cockpit, take out the Very pistol, salute his aircraft, then set it on fire to prevent it falling into enemy hands.

"Didn't want to do it earlier in case I attracted unwanted company," he said as he climbed into the rear cockpit of the Biff. "What kept you?"

"I had to milk Gertrude," said Max, then opened the throttle.

They were almost at the Lines when the Fokkers fell on them. Max heard the pop-pop-pop of their Spandaus, then the chatter of the Vickers behind him as Bentley swung it on its Scarff ring and retaliated.

He kicked the rudder hard and skidded sideways, then gasped as a red-nosed Triplane hurtled past in a ball of fire, its fuel tank obviously ruptured by Bentley's shots.

He saw the other five dive and zoom to get behind and under them, and half-rolled then half-looped to head straight towards them.

He got the lead one in the Aldis sight, cocked the guns and fired, and watched in satisfaction as it dived away, smoke pouring from its engine.

The rest scattered as they hurtled past, and Bentley's Vickers rattled again, then the Huns turned and came back again.

Bloody hell, thought Max, it must be some of the Richthofen crowd. The rest hate taking on Brisfits even more than they do Camels.

He saw another Tripe spin away below them with its engine full on and hit the ground at terrific speed, then winced as a bullet plucked at his sleeve.

He kicked the rudder bar again, knowing that an aircraft skidding sideways was an almost impossible target, and looked over his shoulder to see the Tripe's Spandaus winking as it gave one last burst before veering away from Bentley's lethal fire.

Then turned around to a world of smoke and flame. The last few bullets from the Hun had hit the Brisfit's fuel tank.

Max looked back at Bentley, but he had already seen the horror unfolding before them, then looked down to see where they were. Almost at the Lines, and as if on cue, machinegun fire from the German side arced up to make their impossible situation even worse.

Max suddenly realised that his feet were burning, and looked down to see that the flames were eating through the wooden floor and already licking around the wicker seat on which he sat.

He eased the throttle back, set the rudder pedals to neutral, then undid his safety belt and climbed onto the port wing, one hand clutching a strut and the other holding the joystick to put the aircraft in a sideslip and keep the worst of the flames off them.

There was a rattle like a series of firecrackers going off, and he realised that his own bullets were exploding in the heat.

Bloody marvellous, he thought. I'm just about to shoot myself down.

Out of the corner of his eye, he saw Bentley standing on the revolving stool to stay away from the flames beneath, still firing away.

Max chanced a glance over his shoulder, and saw that the last Triplane had returned to finish them off.

He had never felt so helpless in his life, but the strangest sensation came over him of a calmness in which he realised that he and Bentley were almost certain to die, and he didn't care anymore, not being able to do anything about it.

Suddenly, the floor of Bentley's cockpit burnt through and the stool he was standing fell away. He flung his arms out as he fell, clutched the cockpit rim and managed to get himself braced between it and the Scarff ring, with his legs straddling the fuselage. Thus re-established, he resumed firing.

Faced with such ardent lunacy, the Triplane tilted away, and Max looked down to see that they were over No Man's Land.

He peered vainly ahead through the smoke and flames, which had now set his flying suit on fire, looking for somewhere to land, then glimpsed a stretch of mud between two water-filled shellholes, and aimed for it as best he could.

The Bristol ploughed into the earth, and the last thing Max remembered was sailing through the singed air.

* * *

"I found you face down in a muddy puddle, but at least it put the flames out," said Bentley in the mess that night. "The bloody Huns were still trying to kill us, then a bunch of our lads from the Argyll & Sutherlands scuttled out and saved our bacon. I don't think I've ever been so glad to see men in skirts before."

"I was sure we were dead. I'd actually given up caring. I hope Hobson feels the same about what we did to his Brisfit," said Max as the CO walked in.

"You two win the prize for the most unorthodox flying position of the year. I've just been on to Bristol to tell them they needn't bother with cockpits anymore," he said.

"Oh, and I've put you both down for an MC."

Chapter Nineteen

April 1, 1918

"Congratulations, gentlemen," said Uncle, slamming the mess door against a gust and flicking the rain of his shoulders. "You've all been sacked from the Royal Flying Corps."

"Is this an April Fool?" said Max.

"No, it's retaliation by the brass hats after the Old Man put us down for an MC," said Bentley.

"Neither," said Uncle. "You are now proud members of the new Royal Air Force. So you can get rid of those repulsive castor oil-stained rags you call uniforms and order some lovely new blue-grey jobbies. We get an allowance of 18 quid, apparently. And we can officially wear brown shoes with slacks."

"As opposed to the brown shoes with slacks Bentley is wearing now, do you mean?" said Max.

"Yes, but yesterday they were unofficial, making Bentley an anarchist. Today he is a plodding conformist, like all the rest of us."

"Is that all the good news, Uncle?" said Bentley.

"It is. The bad news is pay will now be in arrears rather than in advance, to stop you dying before you spend it."

"Oh, for God's sake," said Bentley. "Does that mean we lose a month's pay?"

"Almost certainly," said Uncle, handing them both slips of paper. "Which seems like a perfect time to present you with your mess bills."

"Jesus Christ," said Bentley. "Who drank all this?"

April 22, 1918

"They got Richthofen," said Bentley, sticking his head around the door of the hut.

"Oh? That's one for Jonesie. What happened?" said Max, looking up from the book he was reading.

"Canadian called Brown. He can tell you himself. CO's asked him over for dinner. Should be here any time."

Max sighed, and threw aside the book.

"God, I'm in no mood for Tolstoy this evening. A hundred pages and he still hasn't got to the point. Never mind so many characters that you've forgotten who half of them are, and couldn't care less about the other half," he groaned. "Where's that copy of the Illustrated London News you were reading?"

"In my locker."

Max got up, and swung open Bentley's locker, then looked down to see a pile several feet high of silk camisoles, French knickers and drawers, most of them white, with some ivory and a scarlet pair perched on top.

"Bentley, is there something you're not telling me about your underwear habits?" he said.

"What? Oh, those. Souvenirs, so that when I'm old and grey and full of sleep, to quote your compatriot, it will remind me of my lost youth. Or perhaps I shall make a new family flag out of them. Or donate them to the National Gallery."

"Bentley, the more I know you, the stranger you get," said Max, finding the magazine and returning to his camp bed.

"Quite right too. Normality is death," said Bentley, as they heard the sound of an approaching Camel and went outside to see it land.

Brown climbed slowly out of it and walked stiffly towards them. His face was gaunt, his eyes were sunken and bloodshot, and his hair was prematurely grey.

"Sorry, takes me a while. Broke my back crashing a 504 at Chingford. Flying a bed for two months," he said.

"At least you're still walking. Unlike the Baron. Congratulations," said Bentley.

"Not really. When I saw his body earlier, there was a lump in my throat. If he'd been my dearest friend, I couldn't have felt greater sorrow," said Brown.

"It's funny, McCudden said the same thing about Voss," said Max, and told Brown about his last encounter.

"I'm not a bit surprised," said Brown, then stretched his back and looked at the sky.

"You know, it really is a terrible thing to pit kindred spirits against each other."

"The funny thing is," said Brown over dinner that evening, "I'm not even sure I did shoot him down.

"I was up with Wop May, who was at school with me back in Edmonton. I've never lost a pilot in my flight before, and I certainly didn't want to lose Wop, so I'd told him to stay clear of any scrap and watch.

"Anyway, we got into a tangle with Jasta 11 over the Somme and Wop somehow got involved and ended up with Richthofen on his tail right on the deck.

"I shot down to help, fired a quick burst, then had to pull up or crash, so I lost sight of both of them.

"But when I looked at his body earlier today, there was only a single bullet wound from below and the side, and I was behind and above him. Strange, but that's about all I know."

"Strange indeed," said Uncle.

"Say about again," said Bentley.

"Why?" said Brown.

"I just like the way you say it with your accent."

"I haven't got an accent. Everyone else does," said Brown, and they all laughed.

"Have another drink," said Uncle. "Then we'll teach you to say it properly."

"I like it the way it is," said Bentley. "Aboot. Aboot."

"I think Bentley's fallen in love with you, Brown," said Uncle. "Better be careful. He hasn't had his regular medical appointment for at least three days."

"Are you sick?" said Brown.

"Four," said Bentley. "Sadly, yes. I have a rare condition which can only be helped by the tender ministrations of angels of mercy. Aboot."

"Terrible. Any cure?" said Brown.

"Hope not," said Bentley. "Aboot aboot aboot. I think I'm getting the hang of it."

"I wondered which one of us was going to crack first," said Max.

Chapter Twenty

May 21, 1918

Returning from a fairly dull patrol in which Bentley had sent down an Albatros, it suddenly occurred to Max that Yvette was off work, so he gave Bentley a wave then tilted away to fly over her little house.

Yes, there she was, hanging some sheets on the line at the back. He curved low over and waved, and she looked up, her face aglow and her hair blowing in the wind, and waved wildly back.

He was climbing away over the Bois de Roi, the great forest nearby, when a glint of sunlight on metal caught the corner of his eye from among the trees.

"That's strange," he said, and flew back over the forest again, but there was nothing.

That night, he parked the Royal Enfield outside the gate lodge as always, and hugged Yvette on the doorstep.

"Darling, there's just something I want to have a look at, if you don't mind," he said. "I'll be back in half an hour."

They kissed, and he walked off in the direction of the forest, then when he got closer, skirted a hedgerow to the end then peered intently into the gloom beneath the trees.

No, nothing. He must have been imagining things, he thought, then as he turned to walk away, a movement caught his attention. Then another. And another.

Good God, he thought. Good God. There were hundreds, if not thousands, of grey-clad figures in the trees, moving to and fro behind camouflage netting.

"Tunnel," he muttered. "They must have been digging for months."

He took out a notebook, scribbled in it, then crept back along the hedgerow and walked swiftly back to the gate lodge.

"Listen, I'm really sorry, but something's come up. I have to get back to the squadron, and I may not make it back tonight, but if not, I'll see you tomorrow."

Her face fell.

"Oh. I am so sorry. There was something I wanted to tell you."

"Can you tell me now, or will it keep?"

She hesitated, then looked up at him, her face full of love and trust. How beautiful she was, he thought.

"Well, you know I said I would not go all the way with a man before I was married?"

"Yes, I do."

"Well, I think we should. I feel as if we are married anyway, and who knows what will happen in this war, tomorrow or the next day."

He kissed her, then cupped her face in his hands.

"Tomorrow, then," he said.

"Yes, tomorrow. I can't wait."

He hugged her, then walked away, started the Enfield and climbed on.

"Max!" she said, and came running over, and hugged him awkwardly from the side as he sat on the bike. "I love you."

"I love you too," he said, and kissed her again. "Until tomorrow."

"No, forever," she said, and he rode off.

Back at the aerodrome, he told the CO his story.

"Sweet Jesus," said the Old Man. "Do you have the coordinates?"

"Of course. I wrote them down," said Max, then tore the page out of his notebook and handed it over.

The CO looked at it, then picked up the phone.

"Hello? Yes, get me Artillery," he said.

Max looked at his watch. It was too late to go back to Yvette's now. He went to bed, and dreamed of them lying in the buttercup meadow by the river.

He woke, feeling strangely happy, and threw a sock at Bentley.

"Wake up, you lazy bugger. Time to go and shoot some Huns," he said as Bentley groaned and stirred, just as Johnston came in clutching two mugs of tea.

"You're in a chirpy mood this morning for a man who stares death in the face every day," said Bentley, taking a mug. "Something the matter?"

"No, I just had a brief twinge of optimism there. But it soon passed."

"Good thing, too. Highly contagious, optimism."

It was another uneventful patrol. They spotted a brace of Albatri far across the Lines, but the Huns turned away as soon as they spotted the Camels, then they chased a Halberstadt which was several thousand feet higher, and as soon as the observer saw them, the pilot put his nose down and dived for him.

Then they crept up on an observation balloon and sent it down in flames. The sole occupant shook his fist angrily at them as he floated down below his parachute, and Max looked across at Bentley and laughed, then they used up the last of their ammo strafing the German trenches and swept across No Man's Land at twenty feet on the way home.

Max shaved and bathed, then climbed on the Enfield and rode to Yvette's humming Rachmaninov to himself, his heart fluttering as he turned the corner and looked up for the familiar sight of the little gate lodge.

Except the gate lodge was not there. It and the manor house were just piles of smoking rubble from which small wisps of smoke curled up, like sighs of despair.

Max got off the Enfield and stumbled past the shell holes to where he had stood with Yvette the night before, hoping beyond hope. But there was no hope. All hope was gone.

He staggered through the rubble of the gate lodge, and stood there helplessly, then looked down to see a fragment of cloth at his feet. Of white cotton with little Michaelmas daisies on it.

He picked it up, and held it to his face, then buried his head in his hands, and wept like he had never wept before.

Max rode back to the aerodrome, his heart like ice, threw the Enfield down on the grass and walked into the CO's office.

"Nice of you to knock, Edwards."

"Sorry, sir. I've had a bit of a shock. Can I just ask to see the coordinates I gave you for the wood last night?"

"What? Er, yes, here they are."

He handed over a piece of paper, and Max looked at it.

"Yes, those are right. Are they the ones you gave to the artillery?"

"Of course."

"I'm sorry, sir, but can I ask you to check that those are the ones they received?"

"What's this about, boy?" said the CO, then seeing the expression on Max's face, picked up the phone and asked to be put through to Artillery.

"Yes? Hello? I just want to check the coordinates for the shelling of the Bois du Roi last night. Yes, I have them here. Let me read them out. What? Who? I see. Thank you."

He put down the phone.

"Yes, they fell a bit short at first, but soon got it right. So no harm done."

"I see," said Max coldly. "And who was the officer in charge, if you don't mind me asking."

"Who? Oh. Martin, I believe," said the CO.

Chapter Twenty one

May 23, 1918

The Albatros two-seater was sliding in and out of cloud when he saw it, and he used the same cloud as cover to slip effortlessly behind and below it, then raked it with fire.

The propeller stopped, and it began to curve earthward, and he looked over his shoulder to make sure there was nothing around, then followed it down as it sideslipped clumsily over a copse and touched down in a large meadow, then rolled to a halt.

Flames began to creep back from the engine, and the pilot clambered out and dragged the observer free, then pulled him clear from the growing inferno, then stood and looked up at the circling Camel.

Max banked sharply, then tore low back across the meadow until the pilot filled his Aldis sight, then reached for the trigger.

Then took a deep breath, took his finger off it and saw the pilot duck as he soared over his head.

"No," said Max. "No."

He climbed away, his soul drained of feeling, and turned for home, then looked down and realised he was over the road to Amiens along which he had ridden home with Yvette that first night, a lifetime ago. When life had still been possible.

An open-stopped Crossley staff car was racing along it, with an officer lounging in the back seat.

"Fucking brass hats," said Max.

He blipped the engine and slid neatly between the poplars, gliding down behind it, then gunned the engine and swept over it with only feet to spare, rattling off the last of his ammunition for good measure.

The driver looked up, startled, and as Max climbed away, he glanced in his mirror, and saw the Crossley swerve into the ditch and overturn.

"Oh, bollocks," he said.

"Good thing too. Hope he broke his neck, but I won't breathe a word," said Bentley that night in Jack's, then poured another glass of wine and put his hand on Max's forearm.

"Sorry about Yvette, old boy. I know you were a bit attached to her."

"I killed her, Bentley. As surely as if I'd put a gun to her head."

"No, you didn't. You did the right thing. You always do. The people who killed her were the useless bastards who started this Godforsaken caper. They think they rule the world, but they cock up everything they touch."

July 1918

"Congratulations, Edwards," said the CO.

Max opened his eyes and looked up from the sofa in the mess where he was trying and failing to have a nap.

"Why, is he pregnant?" said Bentley.

"Better than that. Distinguished Service Order. Just come through. You get a nice red and blue ribbon to brighten up that crumpled mess you call a uniform."

"Hurrah," said Max.

"Once more with feeling," said Bentley. "This calls for a snifter in Jack's."

"Bloody good idea," said Uncle.

At Jack's, Bentley ordered Bollinger, poured three glasses, and sat down heavily.

"Max, I'm getting seriously worried about you."

"Why?"

"Because your Camel comes back from most patrols more like a flying colander than an aeroplane, chum. Because you're going to get yourself killed if you go on like this. Look at you. You're a mess. Drinking all night, up at dawn, diving into crowds of Huns as if you have some kind of death wish. Which you'll get if you go on like this."

"I don't much care, Bentley, to be honest. My heart's as empty as a weekday church. And my nerves are like a cat playing the piano."

"Don't talk rot. You should be ashamed of yourself. What would Fido do if you went west?" said Uncle.

"Good point. I'd never forgive myself."

"What you needs a spot of rumpy. And possibly pumpy," said Bentley.

"That's your solution to everything," said Max.

"That's because it is the solution to everything. Tell you what, I'll treat you to one of the girls upstairs."

"No."

"Have some more champers. That always makes me frisky."

"Bentley, drying paint would make you frisky," said Uncle.

"Depends on the colour. Besides, I hear they've got a new Japanese girl upstairs. Now that's something I haven't tried. Apparently it's sideways in Oriental women, so you'd have to lie across the bed. Or something."

Max sat there, looking into the middle distance, with hopes, dreams and regrets tearing his heart apart.

"You know what, maybe you're right. Maybe a bit of rumpy and pumpy is what I need," he said.

Bentley patted him on the shoulder.

"That's the spirit. I'll lead you to the den of delight, then while you lay your demons to rest, Uncle and I can finish the rest of this excellent Bollinger, then order another."

He went over to Pierre, handed over some notes, then came back and led Max by the hand across the smoky room then up the creaking stairs.

"Wait here," he said, and went into an adjoining room, then came out a minute later.

"Third on the right. Your Oriental treasure awaits."

He retreated down the stairs, and Max took a step after him. Bentley turned, and wagged a stern finger.

Irresolute and with his heart pounding, Max walked down the corridor, paused, and tapped the third door on the right.

"Entrez, s'il vous plait," said a small voice, and he pushed the door.

A slim, tiny Oriental woman sat on the simple bed wearing a long white nightdress.

"Konbanwa," he said, bowing.

"Pardon?" she said.

"Vous êtes japonaise?"

"Non, chinois. Are you English?"

"Yes. Well, Irish. We're never quite sure."

"My English is better than my French."

"How on earth did you end up here?"

"My husband came here with the Chinese Labour Corps, and I was employed as a translator."

"What happened?"

She bowed her head.

"He was shot for protesting about the conditions. And I was told I was no longer required. This was all that was left for me."

"I am so sorry. Please, can I just give you some money, and go?"

"No, please." She stood, and began to unbutton her nightdress.

In spite of himself, Max felt his groin uncurl.

Afterwards, he clung to her and wept, uncertain whether he was clutching the ghost of Yvette or the shadow of an unattainable future.

"Can you cook?" he said as he buttoned his tunic.

"Pardon?"

"Cook."

"Yes. Of course."

"Wait here."

He went downstairs and walked over to Pierre where he stood behind the bar.

"Pierre, what this place really needs is a more interesting menu," he said.

"Oh?"

"With a more eastern slant. I have a new cook for you. Her name's Hei San. I'll pay her wages, even if all she does is wash dishes."

Pierre shrugged.

"Free staff are always welcome in my establishment," he said, and Max walked back upstairs.

Chapter Twenty two

July 26 1918

Max walked into the mess, threw his Sidcot suit on an armchair, and slumped down after it just as Uncle walked through the door.

"Mannock's gone west," he said.

"What? Bloody hell, I thought he was indestructible. How many kills has he got now?" said Max.

"Had. Sixty one, I think."

"What happened?" said Bentley.

"He and a new boy Inglis shot down an LVG, then Mannock went down to get a look at the wreckage and ran into a 21-gun salute from the lads in the trenches, apparently."

"Ours or theirs?"

"Both, probably. Even after four years of war, those silly bastards in the PBI haven't worked out the difference between a roundel and a cross," said the CO.

August 1918

"Ah, Edwards, bit of an unusual job for you," said the CO as Max closed the door behind him. "This is Sergeant Marnier."

Max turned to find a tough looking middle-aged man in civilian clothes gazing out of the window. He turned, and shook Max's hand.

"Delighted," he said in a slight but perceptible accent.

"The Sergeant is a former NCO in the French Army, but is now engaged in more, er, delicate matters," said Cunningham.

"Ha! He means I am a spy," said Marnier.

"Looks like you've just blown your cover, then," said Max, and Marnier laughed.

"He needs to be dropped over the Lines at dawn tomorrow. Here," said the CO, going to his map table and pointing at a spot about 20 miles behind enemy lines. You can make a note of the coordinates, but he'll point out the exact spot when you get there. You can take my Avro if you promise not to break it. Now let's take him to the mess and give him a nice dinner."

"With English food, that is a contradiction. After you," said Marnier.

At three the next morning, Max was rudely awakened by a tap on the shoulder.

"But soft, what light through window breaks. It is the dawn, and Johnston is the sun," he groaned.

"Morning to you too, sir," said Johnston. "Here's your cuppa. The French bloke says he's ready when you are."

"Have a jolly flight. Send us a postcard if you get caught and shot for transporting spies," said Bentley, then rolled over and went back to sleep.

Max found Marnier standing by the Avro in a flat cap and a large overcoat, the pockets bulging with bread, cheese and a large bottle of wine from the mess that Uncle had donated. At his feet was a large wicker basket.

"Pigeons," said Marnier by way of explanation, although it was hardly needed, what with the faint cooing coming from it.

He climbed awkwardly into the front seat of the Avro, and Max put the basket and the flat cap on his lap and climbed into the back seat, thinking it was the first time he had been in a 504 since Central Flying School. Not to mention the first time since then he'd been involved with pigeons.

“God, another life. Switch off. Suck in,” he said, and at the front of the aircraft, Blythe stopped hugging himself for warmth and turned the propeller.

Half an hour later, Max looked down at the mist-shrouded countryside in the crepuscular half-light before dawn, and Marnier looked back and jabbed his finger at a large meadow.

Max nodded, blipped the engine and began to glide down. As they slid past 100 ft, there was a sudden crack and a bullet whistled past Max’s head. He ducked, and took his thumb off the blip switch to climb away on full throttle. The engine coughed, then picked up, and Marnier looked back.

Max gave him a thumbs up, then jerked his thumb back the way they had come to ask if Marnier wanted to go home.

The Frenchman shook his head vigorously, and pointed to another field half a mile to the left, then pointed at the engine and made a twisting motion to indicate that Max should switch it off so as not to give their welcoming party a chance to follow the sound.

They slid down in a silence broken only by the wind through the wires, whispered across the hedge and descended into the ground mist. He held his breath that there were no rabbit burrows or molehills, and breathed a sigh of relief as they touched down, bounced once then jerked and slithered across the uneven ground.

He climbed out, lifted the pigeon basket out then helped Marnier climb down, and was just about to ask him to swing the prop when a movement out of the corner of his eye caught his attention, and he looked in horror at a dozen grey-clad figures emerging from the woods at the edge of the field.

“Go!” he said to Marnier, knowing that the Frenchman, and possibly both of them, would be shot if caught, and after a moment’s hesitation, Marnier picked up his basket, shook Max’s hand and ran in the opposite direction to the advancing troops.

Now what the hell do I do, thought Max, and the lunatic thought of asking one of the Germans politely to swing the prop for him crossed his mind before he gave a sharp, wild laugh.

I'm going mad. That's what it is, he thought, then pulling off his flying gloves, shoved a finger of each one into the air intakes on either side, pulled the propeller back to suck any excess fuel out of the cylinders, retrieved his gloves, reached into the cockpit, switched on the magneto, and swung the prop.

The engine caught first time, and Max flung himself to the ground, rolled over, lay there as the blades and the wing passed over, then jumped to his feet and raced after the Avro as it bumped across the grass.

Flinging himself at it, he scrabbled at the edge of the cockpit as his flailing boot found and caught the foothold, then hauled himself in and fell heavily on the seat.

He looked up to see that the Germans were now only a hundred yards ahead, and as he gunned the throttle and raced towards them, bullets sang past his head. Something plucked at his sleeve, and there was a crack as the strut beside him splintered, but held.

The running figures grew closer and closer, and he threw his hand across his face and braced himself for the impact as he hauled back on the stick.

Then took his hand away and looked again as the Avro somehow clawed itself into the air and crawled over the heads of the Germans as they flung themselves to the ground.

"Ha! You beauty!" he said, and gave the side of the Avro cockpit a hearty smack, then began to laugh hysterically, then sob.

"Pull yourself together, you silly bastard. You're losing your mind," he said, then looked back at the field at where the Germans were picking themselves up and setting off after Marnier again.

Wheeling the Avro around, he dived back at the field and gave them a rattle with the Lewis gun.

Realising they were caught in the open, they ran back to the shelter of the wood, and after circling for five minutes to give Marnier enough time to get well away, Max climbed to 1000 ft and set for home.

Then sniffed the air, and stuck his head down into the cockpit and sniffed again. Fuel. One of the German bullets must have holed the tank.

"Jesus. Lucky I didn't go up in smoke," he said, then throttled back to a steady cruise, and set course for home.

He was in sight of No Man's Land when the engine stopped. He tried to restart it, then gave up and looked at the muddy wasteland ahead. He might just make it.

The Avro crept down and down, and the German trenches grew closer. Resisting the temptation to pull back on the stick to try and stretch the glide, he kept the nose down and his speed up, and whistled across them at 100 ft, accompanied only by a belated crack from a surprised sentry who looked up at the last minute to see him ghost overhead.

With the world ahead of him churned up by four years of shelling, there was no chance of finding a flat landing spot, and Max picked a thread of ground between two shellholes, and held the Avro thrumming on the brink of the stall to put it down as slowly as possible.

It hit the ground, slithered one way and the other as if it couldn't decide which shellhole to fall into, then came to a halt, having failed to make up its mind either way.

"Bollocks and buggery. This war's going to be the death of me," said Max, hauling himself out of the cockpit as a rattle of machinegun fire from the awakened German trenches cut the air.

He ducked and ran, slipping and sliding and with his mind back for a moment on the dreadful night he had carried young Willy Magee home, and was only a handful of yards away from the British trenches when a rifle appeared over a sandbag, followed by a helmet and a grizzled face.

"Halt, who goes there — friend or foe?"

Max stopped, and his jaw dropped.

"Old Tom, is that you?" he said.

"To be honest, it's been a bit of a boring war," said Tom over a mug of tea. "I've spent all of it on sentry duty. Or cleaning my rifle. The only exciting thing that happened was back in April, I was shelling a hard-boiled egg and trying to clean the rifle at the same time, and I dropped it."

"What, the egg?"

"God, no. Too bloody precious. The rifle. Unfortunately I had a round in the spout and it went off just as that Hun chap in the red outfit went past, hotly pursued by one of your lads."

"Who, Richthofen?"

"That's the one. The Red Baron, they called him. Anyway, I read in the Wipers Times that he'd crashed just after that, so your lad must have got him."

"That's not what Brown says," said Max.

"And then just last month I was having a nice cup of tea when a whizz-bang went off right where you were just now. Frightened me so much I dropped the brew right in my goolies, knocked my rifle and send a round skywards just as one of your lads passed over. I do hope I didn't do any damage."

"What date was that, do you remember?" said Max.

"It was the 26th. I remember, because it was my birthday. Ah, here's a despatch rider. He can give you a lift back to your aerodrome."

Max finished his tea and bounced back home on the pillion of the Phelon & Moore, fairly certain that old Tom had gained the unique distinction of downing the leading air aces of both sides without knowing a thing about it.

And even more certain that he was going to get a complete bollocking from the CO when he told the Old Man where he'd parked his Avro.

"Ah, you're back. Jolly trip?" said Bentley as Max walked into their hut that evening to find him carefully packing his impressive selection of silk underwear into a large duffel bag

"Very," said Max. "Where are you going with those?"

"Taking them to Madame Voillet. Remember that family flag I was thinking of? It will fly from the battlements of Priory Towers when this cursed war is over."

Chapter Twenty three

November 9, 1918

"You hardly ever see any Huns stooging about these days. Think they're all on holiday?" said Bentley.

"Don't knock it. If I never see another Fokker as long as I live, it won't be a moment too soon. Especially those new D.VIIs. They're too sharp for my liking," said Max, pouring another glass of Château Margaux, then looking at the label. "Bloody hell, it's a 1911. I thought those were long gone."

"Your lovely Oriental friend makes sure Pierre keeps a few behind. A small gesture for what you did for her. And paying her wages," said Uncle as Hei San brought over three steaming plates, kissed Max on the cheek and set them on the table.

"Thank you, Hei San," said Max, and she squeezed his shoulder and walked away.

"Mmm, slow-roasted pork belly. Yum and double yum. Oh, and that stopped ages ago. Pierre's too decent. He's been paying her since then."

"Good food, good wine and good women," said Bentley. "I shall be glad when this bloody war is over and I can get back to that holy trinity of civilised pleasures."

"Bentley, you never left them," said Max. "Pass the rice."

November 10, 1918

They crossed the line at 20,000 ft the next morning, and Max huddled in his cockpit. He seemed to feel the cold much more these days, he thought, then scanned the sky out of long practice, although as Bentley had said in Jack's last night, you hardly ever saw a Hun in the sky these days.

Dear Bentley. He looked across at his oldest and best friend in the world, and Bentley looked back, stuck out his tongue, thumbed his nose and waggled his fingers.

Max threw his head back, and laughed. It seemed like several lifetimes ago that he had walked into the hut at Upavon to see him lying there on the camp bed, with one hand behind his head and the other clutching a copy of *Punch*.

They had been other people then. And he had been another person before, first at Termon, then at Finner, and then through the awful months in the trenches. Or maybe there was the same person in there, something fundamental that didn't change, through all our lives until we die.

If we get the chance, that is, his thoughts turning to Jim Kilpatrick, drowning in the yellow fluid that filled his lungs. Or John Jameson, screaming in agony as he burned for someone to shoot him. And Adam, who shot his father, and could not bear it, and then they shot him for not bearing it.

And Lowry. And McMahon. And young Willy Magee, whose single eye looking at him then past him into a lost future haunted him still at times, in the hollow of the night when he could not sleep.

Jonesie, falling and burning and falling and burning.

Yvette. Dear, sweet, lovely Yvette, in her Michaelmas daisy dress and his jacket, hugging him close on the Enfield on the road from Amiens. Lifting her nightdress over her head to reveal her pale, slender beauty that first night. Or unbuttoning his shirt, in a sunlit buttercup meadow by the river.

And her parents, so kind to him.

So many good people, gone.

Please God, soon this will all be over, and I will go home again, to walk with Fido in the Glen and find what has not changed in me. What is still human, somewhere in there. And K —

His thoughts were interrupted by a sound like tearing calico, and he jumped in alarm as his mirror shattered.

To his right Bentley's Camel soared and fell away, pursued by a pair of Fokker D.VIIs covered in multicoloured lozenges.

"Jesus. Jesus," he said, and fell after them. He caught one and sent it spiralling down, and had almost caught the other when he saw the dread sight of petrol vapour streaming back from Bentley's engine.

The Fokker filled his sights, and he gave it a long burst from the twin Vickers. The pilot sat bolt upright, then slumped, and the aircraft began to spin, slowly then more rapidly as it fell in a last long descent to earth.

Max watched it go, then turned to where Bentley's Camel was still falling, trailing a stream of white vapour.

And then Max's heart stopped as a lick of yellow flame crept back towards the cockpit.

"No. Please God no. Not Bentley," he said, as his dearest friend stood up in the cockpit, saluted, then jumped.

Max watched in despair as the figure tumbled over and over.

And then, as suddenly and surprisingly as a magician pulling a bouquet out of his pocket, there came a blossoming of silk.

Silk which was mostly white, with some ivory patches, and in the middle a splash of scarlet.

"Bentley. Oh, Bentley, you mad, wonderful bastard," said Max, then laughed and cried and laughed again all the way home.

Chapter Twenty four

April 1919. Carrickmore station

Max rolled his Royal Enfield down the ramp from the goods carriage onto the platform, and rode it down Main Street as Pat Rafferty and Seamus McGarrity came walking up.

"Let me hazard a guess," said Seamus. "Young Master Edwards."

"Not so young as when he left us," said Pat. "You're a great colour."

"Posted to Palestine straight after the war ended. Couldn't even get home for Christmas," said Max.

"Ah, yes the campaign against the Turks," said Pat. "We read about it in the *Con*. Bit warmer than the Western Front, at any rate. So many young lives lost."

"Yes. Complete bloody mess, the whole thing," said Max.

"It's good to see you home, Max," said Seamus.

"It's good to be home, Seamus. Good to be home," said Max, then shook their hands and rode down the hill and round the corner, past his old primary school and the back gate lodge, then on to the Bush.

Turning off the road, he rode past the front gate lodge and up the lane past the Water Meadow and the Devil's Wood, in which the rooks cawed as if the war of men and machines had never been.

He stopped the bike outside the archway into the big yard, cut the engine, got off and stood there for a moment, then reached into his pocket.

He took out the little bag of lilac silk and slid Kumiko's carp into his palm, looked at it for a few seconds, then put it back in the bag and returned it to his pocket.

All the workers were in the fields, and the silence hung in the bright spring air.

A silence which was broken at that moment by a loud "ARF!" He turned to see a maelstrom of black and white hurtling towards him, and the next thing he knew, he was flat on his back, his face being scoured by a warm, wet tongue.

"Fido! Good to see you too, chum," he said, running his hands through the warm fur and breathing in the smell of warmth, life and endless love.

He got to his feet and stood there for a moment looking into the yard with Fido leaning against his leg, then decided that before he went in to see his parents, he would walk down to the lake. With Fido trotting by his side looking up at him to make sure he never left again, he turned right past the hay barn and rounded the corner of the sawmill, then stopped.

The path to the lake was now an avenue of cherry blossoms, bobbing in the mild breeze.

He walked down it in wonder, and stopped on the lake shore. On the island stood a single maple tree, and on the shore, a simple hut made of cedar.

He opened the door. White walls, a wooden floor. On a small table in the middle, an indigo vase and a yellow chrysanthemum.

As he stood there, a squall came from nowhere, tearing apart the surface of the lake and filling the air with a flurry of pink blossom.

He turned, and Kumiko emerged from the storm of petals, in a silk dress the colour of graphite. His heart stopped, at the sight of her.

"Max-san!" she said, and stopped. "You are a man."

He laughed, and bowed.

"Kumiko-san. It is so good to see you. Is the Major at home?"

She looked at him, a ripple of conflicting emotions passing across her face, and then it was still.

"No. You have not heard?"

"Heard what?"

"He died. His car was found overturned in a ditch in France. It was unmarked, so no one knew what happened. His neck was broken, and he died instantly."

"Kumiko, I am so sorry. I knew nothing of this. When did it happen?"

"It was the 23rd of May last year."

He looked at her, breathing hard.

"What about the driver?"

"The strangest thing. He was knocked unconscious, but remembered nothing of what happened."

Max looked up at the perfect rainwashed blue of the spring sky, then back at her. The squall had gone as quickly as it passed, and a single cherry blossom settled in her hair. She brushed it off.

"Are you sorry?"

"I should be."

She looked across the lake to where a crane flapped lazily across the mirrored flat, accompanied by its perfect reflection.

"But I am not."

He looked at her. He had forgotten how astonishing her eyes were.

"It is very good to see you again, Max-san. Very good."

"It is very good to see you too, Kumiko-san. It is, in fact, better than heaven."

"Oh. How so?"

He took a deep breath.

"Because I did not have to die to love you."

She looked at him for a long time, her face as serene as the lake reflected in her eyes.

And then she took his hand. And life began.

Epilogue

June 1920

Max and Kumiko sat on a cedar bench at the edge of the lake, looking at the reflection of the sun setting on the still water. Her head lay against the hollow of his neck, and his hand lay on hers where it rested on her swollen belly.

Fido lay at their feet, then raised his head and cocked an ear, and behind them they heard the sound of a motor car making its way down the avenue of cherry blossom trees.

Max turned, and saw Bentley waving from a large midnight blue open-topped limousine.

"Very impressive, Bentley. What on earth is it?" said Max.

"A Bentley, of course," laughed Bentley. "The very first one. None of the other customers have got theirs yet, but you remember Gallop of 56 Squadron? Came over one night and got stinko?"

"Vaguely. Long, thin face and big ears?"

"That's the one. Well, he designed the engine, so he sneaked this one out early. Kumiko! You're looking swell. In every sense," laughed Bentley as Max noticed the small silk pennant fluttering from the chrome rod on the mudguard. White and ivory stripes, with a flash of scarlet.

"Very good, Bentley. Very good," he said, as all three hugged.

"Arf," said Fido, who as a collie always had to have the last word.

Appendix I: acknowledgments

Termon is very real. My grandfather Edward was the butler there, and he and my grandmother Maria, their five children and their dog Fido lived in rooms above the coach house which I have used as the home of Max and his parents.

Growing up, I saw Termon from the side of the butler, the footman, the blacksmith, the estate manager and the farm labourers who were summoned at noon every day by the tolling of the coach-house bell.

As they came in one by one from the fields, the open fireplace in the long stone room by the gate into the big yard was already ablaze and a large black pot filled with potatoes swung over it.

The men sat themselves on wooden benches down each side of the room, and the potatoes were ladled out onto newspaper on the floor in front of them, eaten in their hands, with salt and butter.

The pot was replaced by a kettle just as black and the tea was made. They would light their pipes, take a mug of sweet and milky tea, throw the leavings into the remains of the fire and return to the fields.

It was far from the comfortable life on the other side of the scullery door, through which my grandfather passed twice a day on his way to and fro between two worlds.

As a child, I saw little of life on the other side of that scullery door. Occasionally, when the family was away, my grandfather would take me on a tour of the house, an experience of giddying possibilities which probably gave me my aspiration for the sort of civilised life which in cities — since growing up in the country gave me an abiding fear of green fields — can only be lived in grand Victorian town houses with book-lined rooms.

The Major is entirely fictional, although some of the staff and workers in Termon and Carrickmore are borrowed from my own memory and a brief essay by Desmond Hill on his memories of Termon.

Desmond, no relation, was the son of Professor Sir Geoffrey Hill, the acclaimed aeronautical engineer who according to my father used to arrive at Termon in a giant Studebaker limousine, and whose tailless Pterodactyl glider hung from the roof of the turf house in the big yard for years.

Desmond, who went on to be a Spitfire pilot after the Second World War and the RAF's youngest Comet jet pilot, got in touch with me after I visited Termon with my wife Cate and wrote the articles in the News Letter reproduced in Appendix II, and we became close friends with him and his wife Belinda and visited them for dinner several times in their home in Holywood.

Both, sadly, have passed away, although we remain good friends with their children Richard and Leanda.

Before Desmond died, I drove him down to Termon for a look around, but the Alexanders had long gone, driven out by a bullet in the post as a warning from the IRA who have always been prevalent in the area, and it was already a sad place, boarded up and heading inexorably towards dereliction, although it was the scene for a remarkable event which I still cannot explain.

Desmond took a photograph of me making a note beside the front door which my grandfather would have opened to receive guests, and when it was developed, standing only a few yards in front of me was the distinct figure of a white-haired man in a three-piece black suit who was the image of my grandfather.

As I say, I cannot explain it, but a shiver ran down my spine when I saw it, as it does even now as I write this.

With the house boarded up and the gardens and Glen overgrown, Termon was placed on the Department of the Environment's buildings at risk register in 2012.

In Carrickmore, I have backdated McGarrity's to the Edwardian era. Rafferty's would have been there then, but has now closed after 100 years in existence.

Somme sources

The Road to the Somme. Men of the Ulster Division tell their story by Philip Orr

RFC and Luftstreitkräfte sources

Avro 504 aficionados will notice that I have simplified the starting and flying process, particularly the use of the block tube and fine adjustment levers, since those alone would have taken up several hundred pages. And possibly the rest of my life.

Others will have endless hours of enjoyment discovering which bits I have nicked and adapted from the following, as well as websites too countless to mention:

The Royal Flying Corps in World War I by Ralph Barker.

The Royal Flying Corps 1914-1918 by Peter G Cooksley.

Aces' Twilight. The War in the Air 1918 by Robert Jackson

Fighter Tactics and Strategy 1914-1970 by Edward H Sims

Sagittarius Rising by Cecil Lewis.

Winged Victory by VM Yeates.

Every Biggles book ever written, and I have virtually all of them, particularly *Biggles Learns to Fly*, *Biggles of 266* and *Biggles of the Camel Squadron.*

By Jove, Biggles! The Life of Captain WE Johns by Peter Beresford Ellis and Piers Williams

I'm also hugely grateful to David Bremner, the chairman of the British Microlight Aircraft Association and my predecessor as editor of *Microlight Flying* magazine, for invaluable advice on First World War aircraft and the aviation history of the era, not to mention proof reading the first draft and putting me right on several inaccuracies.

David, his brother Rick and friend Theo Willford have built and flown a replica of the brothers' grandfather's Bristol Scout after finding the original control stick, rudder bar and magneto in his workshop after he died. For a history of the project, see https://bristolscout.wordpress.com/.

My fascination with Werner Voss stems from when I spent six weeks of the school summer holidays when I was sixteen building a 1/72nd scale model of the Albatros described in the book, down to the flying controls in the cockpit made of fuse wire and the red heart and laurel wreath on the fuselage, painstakingly painted with a very fine brush, a pin and a magnifying glass.

Only for my cousin to wreck it by throwing it across the living room to see if it could fly.

I will forgive him. Eventually.

Appendix II: News Letter columns on Termon, 2002

One

"Catherine," I said as we leaped out of bed and pulled back the curtains to reveal a perfect summer's morning, "today we are going to Termon."

Termon, as regular readers will know, is the big house where my grandfather Edward was the butler, and on whose estate I spent my childhood.

We lived about a mile away, in a house with no electricity or running water, and all I had to play with was a stick. And it was broken. I have told Cate this often, but she does not quite believe me for some strange reason.

At last I was going to prove it to her, I thought as we drove through Omagh. I pointed out thrilling sights like the hospital where I was born, Omagh Academy, the grammar school I went to, and the playing fields down by the river where we played rugby in the winter, cricket in the spring and soccer on balmy summer evenings.

Then we were on the road to Carrickmore. How well I remembered it, for even after we moved to Omagh, when I was thirteen, every summer weekend I would cycle the ten miles back to Termon, where my grandmother Maria lived with my aunt after my grandfather died, to walk by the pond, play soccer in the Water Meadow, help the workers with the hay and explore the Glen.

We turned right before Carrickmore, down the Quarry Road and right at the Bush, over the old railway bridge and right at the remains of Nine Mile House, once an overnight inn for the Belfast to Dublin stagecoach.

I stopped the car at the gate and got out, and there was the field, surrounded by tall trees and flanked by a babbling brook, where in the Fifties my father had turned an Army surplus Nissen hut and a pile of planks into both a home called Meadowbrook for his new bride and the world headquarters of Mid-Ulster Motors, the little garage he ran.

In front of us was the gravel drive where I was photographed in short trousers, satchel and cap, leaving for my first day at school.

Beyond that was the garage where crippled Nortons and Triumphs would be coaxed back to life, then the kitchen door, a living room with an ancient battered leather sofa and a stove — in front of which we were washed in a tin bath every Saturday night.

Beyond that a bedroom, where, in bed for two months with bronchitis as a ten-year-old, I spent my days in Eagles annuals and Biggles books.

On our right was the snowdrop bank where dad's old Castrol sign turned in the breeze. Further right was my mother's kitchen garden, and the trees where she was not adverse to stepping out of the front door with my father's .22 and potting a pigeon for supper. Beyond that was the hill where I remembered sledging straight into a whin bush one winter and at the top of the hill Ellen Lowry's cottage, where she lived alone with two mad dogs.

Behind the house was an outside toilet, and the spot where I once lit a fire and stood in the smoke to test a gas mask dad had brought home, emerging black from head to foot.

To the left were the sheds where our collection of hens and ducks, cats, dogs and pigs lived, all trotting over when we arrived home from school to be variously scratched and stroked. Pinky and Perky, Goosey and Joxer. I remembered them all.

So many memories, and now, only the long grass waving in the sun.

"Are you all right, love?" said Cate, taking my arm.

"Sorry, dear," I said, wiping away a manly tear. "We may never find the broken stick in all this."

At last we got back into the car and drove away from Meadowbrook, past Tyrooney Orange Hall and up the concrete road to Carrickmore.

This was the road where my mother had taken us in our first car, a black Ford Popular with pop-up trafficators. As she approached the giddy speeds of 30 mph, we screamed and begged her to slow down.

Outside Termonmaguirke Primary School, where I had taken my first steps on the long road of education, an old man with white hair was sitting on the wall, on his face the gentleness you rarely see in city folk.

Something made me stop the car and walk back to him.

"I know who you are, Geoffrey," he said, holding out his hand before I spoke. "Willy Dixon. I worked at Termon for twenty years." Indeed, he did, for there were three of them: Big Long Willy, Willy the mason and Willy the gardener.

His son and daughter-in-law, Harry and Violet, came out and shook our hands, and then we were invited in for a cup of tea, in a quiet room where the clock ticked, the *News Letter* sat on the sofa and the window looked out over Drumlister, the townland where WF Marshall famously complained that he was clabber to the knee.

This being the country, of course, a cup of tea did not just mean a cup of tea. It meant two trays piled with wheaten bread, fruit loaf, cheese, jam and several species of chocolate biscuits, and it was some time later that we staggered to the car, shook hands once again and drove up to the village of Carrickmore.

My aunt Muriel, who had taken over as sexton of Termonmaguirke parish from her late husband Billy, had gone off driving with my visiting mother. Perhaps they were at the Foam Disco advertised on a hall halfway up the street.

"They never had foam discos in my day, dear," I said to Cate as I took her hand and we walked in to the grassy graveyard to find the graves of my grandfather Edward, my grandmother Maria and their daughter Harriet, who died of meningitis when she was nine.

All was still, and there was no sign of life, either, at Pat Rafferty's, the village shop where my mother had taken me to buy my first rugby boots for Omagh Academy.

From the cavernous depths at the back of the shop, Pat had produced a pair of football boots whose box indicated proudly that this particular model had been worn and approved by Stanley Matthews.

Today, there was a Thunderbirds outfit sitting behind the yellow cellophane in the window, just as there had been when I was a boy, and as I walked down the street, everything seemed to slip backwards in time.

Outside McGarrity's, the sign had not changed in forty years, and as I opened the door, the bell still tinged.

A box of turnips sat on the floor, there was a handwritten price list for tobacco on the wall and there, standing in front of a shelf of glass jars of clove rock, brandy balls and gobstoppers, was Mr McGarrity himself.

"Let me hazard a guess," he smiled. "Young Geoffrey Hill."

I looked at him, astonished. The last time I had been in that shop must have been thirty six years ago, buying a Crunchie bar.

"It is indeed," I said at last.

"Well, well, well," he said. "And what'll it be?"

I bought some gobstoppers and wandered out into the street to find Cate looking up at a pair of circling crows.

"Are you all right?" she said, for the second time that day.

"Not really. I'm just astonished to be grown up," I said. "Fancy a gobstopper?"

We drove down the road from Carrickmore, and turned left at the second of the two Termon gate lodges, where after hay making as a boy I was always treated to blue and white striped mugs of sweet, milky tea and thick white bread and jam sandwiches.

Twice a week as a boy I would cycle up this very same lane on the blue and white Vincent bicycle I got for passing my eleven-plus, past the Water Meadow then a bit faster past the haunted Devil's Wood and the Runner, wheel into the big yard then the small one, and run up the stone stairs to watch Blue Peter on an ancient black and white Ferguson TV which had been handed down from the big house.

Just over the horizon was the bog where in summer we would cut turf for the winter, stopping at one for tomato sandwiches my mother had made. I always saved one until we got home that night, loving the way the flavour had soaked into the bread.

And down to our left was the start of the garden wall, behind which we had gorged ourselves on gooseberries, strawberries and apples straight from the bush.

"I'm surprised I didn't turn into Billy Bunter," I said as we got out of the car beside the first of the outbuildings. This was the one where the workers, called from the fields by the noon bell, would sit on two benches along the walls for their midday meal of potatoes boiled in a black pot over an open fire and eaten from newspapers on the stone floor with salt.

I had sat amongst their legs, a forest of rough tweed and muddy boots, listening to tales of the fields and hedgerows as they took their pipes and mugs of tea afterwards.

Beyond that, through a stone arch, was the outer yard, surrounded by stables, tack rooms, a workshop where I was lost among smells of leather and oil, the coach house and outside it the pump where my grandmother drew water.

Beyond was the inner yard, and the pantry door where every evening my grandfather, his work finished for the day, would emerge, spit on the cobbles and march across whistling to climb the steps to the rooms above the coach house for his own supper where it sat bubbling on the range. Although not before he had spread a newspaper on the floor and polished his brogues, watched intently by his dog Fido.

We opened a gate and walked around the gardens gone wild. Here were the trees which, as Willy Dixon had said, my father and his brother Freddie would always be found at the tops of. And here was the oak which all the estate children would climb when the big house had a ball, to gaze in at a finery which would be forever denied to them.

Today it was denied to us as well, for the windows to the ballroom were shuttered and broken, their eyes empty to the past and to an unspoken future.

The Alexanders, the Anglo-Irish family who filled its gracious rooms, are all gone now, after bullets in the post and dark threats on midnight telephones.

Finally bought by an optimistic and empathetic builder called Malachy Rafferty, it was for a time an equestrian centre, but now the future of the old house is as uncertain as the wind which blows through its broken windows.

"If we win the lottery, dear, we will turn it into a grand country house hotel," I said to Cate as we walked by the sawmill, down by the lake, past the standing stones and down the Glen, which in my childhood was the American West, the Amazon and the jungles of Africa rolled into one unexplored darkness.

But even the Glen was overgrown, and we made our way painstakingly back to the car.

What would that young boy, who once played and ran in these golden fields, have thought of the man who now stood below the stone arch in the evening light and wondered how his childhood and youth had gone so quickly?

He would have been quite pleased, I hope. And gratified to know that when not quite so young Geoffrey Hill returned to his grand town house in Belfast, he sat down, spread a newspaper on the floor and polished his brogues in front of the range, just as his grandfather had done.

Two

The column I wrote recently on Termon, the big house near Carrickmore where my grandfather, Edward, was a butler, has generated a wonderfully civilized flurry of interest from people who knew him and my grandmother, Maria.

The sort of people who take the time to sit down and write a beautifully composed letter with a fountain pen rather than dash off a text message saying RU2 CMNG 2 DNR?

People like Desmond Hill, whose family were related to the Alexanders who owned Termon, and who would arrive for summer and Christmas holidays in a large Studebaker limousine owned by his father, Professor Sir Geoffrey Hill, who invented the flying wing and kept a prototype glider in the turf house at Termon.

Although I never met him, the fact that we share a name must have kept his love of aeroplanes hanging in the still air at Termon down the years until I appeared there on a Vincent bicycle, wearing a red pullover and an expression of baffled optimism, and absorbed that love from the air into my heart so that I had no choice but to finally become a pilot myself.

"There would be twenty six of us children there at Christmas, running riot in the house," Desmond said one evening last week after he and his wife Belinda invited us out to Holywood for dinner in a home where the fire crackled, dogs slept, ancient paintings lined the walls and the air was gentle and bright with manners which had been polished so beautifully over the years that they were hardly there at all.

"Your grandfather was wonderful at keeping order and guiding us away from grown-up disputes in the drawing room, but he was splendid at keeping us entertained as well; one Christmas Eve he let loose a rabbit in the bedrooms and we were almost sick with laughter trying to catch it."

It was a world I had only seen from the other side of the scullery door, which my grandfather always slammed as the conclusion to his working day, after he had served the last port after dinner.

From where I sat by the front window of the rooms he and my grandmother shared above the coach house, I could hear his footsteps click slow and easy across the cobbled small yard, then up the stone steps and home for the late supper which my grandmother had warming for him on the range.

Through the arched gateway by their front door there was a bigger yard, surrounded by stables, tack rooms rich with leather and brass, workshops and the coach house where, when no one was looking, I would climb aboard the Alexander family limousine, grasp the large wooden steering wheel and go on journeys which would go as far as my imagination would take me, to fabled lands which existed only in my head and what I had learnt from books

Every so often, the family would host grand balls to which the great and good of the county would arrive by horse and carriage and be decanted into the ballroom to dance the night away.

The footmen would be taken away to spend the evening in the servant's quarters, and the children of the estate, my father among them, would climb the great oak tree in the garden and spend the night gazing in through the ballroom windows, the light of many jewels dancing on their faces among the leaves.

I raised my glass as Desmond poured me another after-dinner malt and, in the same light dancing in the crystal, saw at that moment that I was balancing elegantly on a tightrope between two worlds.

THE END

20827116R00097

Printed in Great Britain
by Amazon